# THE WEED KILLER

# GEORGE MURRAY

Grosvenor House
Publishing Limited

# THE WEED KILLER

Is the intellectual property of the author
GEORGE MURRAY
All rights reserved 1990 © George Murray

Cover design by
PAULA HÖRLING-MOSES
www.macmoses.net

Cover photos by
www.shutterstock.com

Published by
GROSVENOR HOUSE PUBLISHING LIMITED
28–30 High Street
Guildford, Surrey
GU1 3EL
August 2015
www.grosvenorhousepublishing.co.uk

ISBN 978-1-78148-960-4

The novel is entirely a work of fiction.
The names, characters and incidents portrayed in it are
the work of the author's imagination. Any resemblance to actual
persons, living or dead, events or localities is entirely coincidental.

# PROLOGUE

This story of crime fiction is set in the west highlands of Scotland and introduces Andrew Fleming, a dedicated police officer who has moved to the region on the grounds of raising his family in a healthier environment. He sees the surrounding area as a garden of natural beauty and the indigenous population as healthy and moral.

His instincts draw his attention to certain discrepancies in the local scene. Incoming strangers have not come to the notice of the police generally but Fleming senses that a criminal network is at work. He pursues his suspicions without any substantive support from the local Chief Inspector who does not wish to see any local police officer raising hares that cannot be caught.

Fleming's enquiries and surveillance eventually expose matters sufficiently for him to report his findings of drug importation to a higher level. There is support from senior officers but no local assistance given, only an arrangement for him to report further developments to these senior officers until a clear opportunity arises for an operation to be launched.

The criminals involved are spread throughout the United Kingdom and Fleming builds a list of contacts with local knowledge of those apparently involved elsewhere in the country. Police activity and treachery among the leading suspects of drug trading leads to murder and theft of funding. This sparks action in those under Fleming's watchful eye and he realises that matters have come to a head. He is aware of the arrival of two leading players in the drugs conspiracy. One has stolen the cash and is seeking to escape. The other has been robbed by the first man and is seeking to kill him.

Fleming reports matters to senior officers but then seizes a chance to deal with the matter himself. When he does he creates his biggest secret and will never tell another human being what he has done. He fails to tell his wife exactly what action he took, of course, but he does reveal to her and the reader, his personal motivation.

# ONE

The small trawler rocked gently in the darkness. The sky was overcast with high cloud but, unusually for the Scottish seas west of Mull, there was no wind at all.

Kneeling on the floor of the tiny cabin Fergus Morrison searched through the wiring beneath the control switches for the loose connection that had brought about the lighting failure. Behind him his young crew of Jamie Cameron and Roddy McCuish followed the torch beam with supporting interest. This type of situation was not something new. The boat itself was over fifty years old and there was always some wee thing going wrong. It was all a part of the life that Fergus had come to love.

It was now twenty years since he realised that a career in accountancy was not for him and he had escaped the rat race to find the tranquillity of the west highland coast. Since his first casual acceptance of a berth on board a fishing vessel he had entertained no thoughts of being anything other than a fisherman. Clever saving and investment of hard earned income had enabled him to purchase the 'Beacon Belle' and now he was delighted to be able to offer young Jamie and Roddy an introduction to the life he had enjoyed. Fergus had been too much of an individual to have ever considered marriage and these young men were the only kind of family he knew. He had no social life to speak of and his only link with his past was the occasional letter he exchanged with an old school friend.

As he reached each taped connection, Fergus pulled gently at it to ensure that it held firm. With no hint of impatience, he stopped to roll a cigarette. Roddy took the opportunity to step outside and stretch himself.

"I can hear an engine, skipper." Roddy said quietly. Fergus had cut the engine of the Beacon Belle to avoid vibration and now, in the darkness with no running lights, the black hull of his boat would be virtually invisible. He rose and stepped outside.

"Aye. A big boat coming from the south west but she must be over a mile away." considered Fergus, completing his cigarette. "Pass me the glasses, Jamie."

Looking through the binoculars Fergus could see most of the approaching vessel as she was illuminated by her own lights. It appeared to be a large trawler, about an eighty footer. He continued to watch the trawler as she drew closer but then she suddenly cut her lights and her engines.

"That's queer." remarked Roddy.

"Aye it is," agreed Fergus, "But at least she should not come too close without her engines."

"Listen." whispered Jamie sharply, turning his head to the south east. "Another engine."

This second engine noise was different. It was the powerful inboard petrol engine of a fast planing craft.

"And this bugger has no lights either." remarked Fergus quietly, realising that the second vessel was sufficiently close that her running lights should have been obvious. "She sounds as if she's heading for the trawler."

Looking through the binoculars, Fergus could just make out the pale shadow of a GRP hull approximately forty foot long.

The fast craft cut her throttle then her engine. From her forward cabin a strong lamp sent three flashes towards the larger boat. In the lamplight Fergus could see that the large trawler was Jersey registered with an orange painted hull.

He recognised this trawler. He had seen it often in the area in the past six months. The vessel had unloaded fish at the northern ports which suggested that she had been fishing the ocean waters to the north west of Scotland. On the face of it there was nothing too unusual about this activity but something about this particular boat had aroused Fergus's suspicion. He had never said as much to his young crew but, in the hope of sounding topical and interesting, he had mentioned it in his most recent letter to his old school friend.

"Did ye hear that?" whispered Jamie as the sound of a splash reached them from the vicinity of the larger vessel. This sound was immediately followed by three lamp flashes from the trawler before her heavy diesels roared back into life. The trawler then turned south, neglecting to switch on her lights.

Fergus lifted his binoculars and peered at the spot where the large trawler had been.

"A big marker buoy." he reported evenly, answering the unspoken question on the lips of his crew.

The white hulled vessel started her engine and idled forward to the marker buoy. Fergus watched through his glasses once more but sensed rather than saw that the marker buoy was being lifted from the water. The engine revs increased and the white hull rose into a planing position and set off at speed in a south easterly direction still showing no light. Fergus quickly surveyed the area of white wash left by the fast craft.

"Aye. Just as we thought. The marker buoy has gone."

"What do you suppose they were doing?" enquired Roddy in slightly dramatic tone.

"They were certainly transferring something from the big trawler to that flying machine," answered Fergus, "and judging by the way they did it I don't think it was legal merchandise."

"What do you think it was, skipper?" young Jamie asked.

"Could have been anything, guns, drugs, just anything at all."

"Good job for us they never saw us." observed Roddy.

"Aye. There's something in what you say." mused Fergus, casting an eye towards his radio and small radar scanner both of which were, for the time being at least, switched off. "Come on, boys, let's get these lights fixed."

It was almost an hour later before Fergus finally detected the fault and was able to switch on the lights of the Beacon Belle. He started up the engine and switched on his ships radio. He also turned on an old wireless set which provided acceptable music from some foreign station.

Beneath a strong white light shining aft, Roddy and Jamie sat on boxes and began to bait up some set lines with mackerel pieces. Once baited the lines would again be set to take the dogfish.

Jacques Troutam had only gone a few miles south before stopping again. He pushed a podgy right hand up into his full dark beard as he gazed down at the small blip on his radar screen. He could not recall having seen it on the previous visits and the chart gave no possible explanation. If it had been a boat he would surely have seen its lights or heard its engine. For almost an hour now the object had not moved perceptibly from its original position. It was unlikely to be a boat and he did not feel like going back just to satisfy his curiosity.

If it was not a boat then it was not something to worry about, not anything to threaten him or his low-life crew in their dark and disguised, but lucrative, business.

He stepped outside to the deck, taking with him a powerful set of binoculars. By way of a final gesture to his own curiosity he peered through the binoculars more towards than at the spot where he had dropped the marker buoy and creel.

As he saw nothing but darkness he smiled in scorn at his own concern but suddenly the smile faded. In the centre of the darkness a white light had appeared and, as he adjusted the glasses, a red port light became visible. It was a boat. His face tightened and his thick hands threatened to crush the binoculars.

He stamped back into his cabin and looked at his radar screen. Now there was movement. The boat was on a southerly heading towards him.

Troutam still had no running lights and he again cut his engines. As he watched the gradual approach of the Beacon Belle his rage grew inside him. The previous fixed position of the boat meant that the crew must have seen him make the exchange. They might well have noted the identity of the boats. There had been nothing on the radio but they would probably wait to report the matter ashore. Whoever this boat was it was now a threat to Jacques Troutam and he was not about to be retired out of such easily earned bounty.

More from cunning than patience Troutam waited until the small trawler was about to pass within a hundred metres of him before his huge fist turned his ignition switch and then pushed the throttle full toward.

Fergus could hear nothing but the heavy German marching song from the old wireless set and the sound of his own engine. Behind the cabin the young crew joked with each other about their skipper's taste in music, shouting above the sound of the Beacon Belle's engine. They were not looking and could not readily see beyond the beam of the strong deck light but the sound of a heavy engine beat, close to, made them turn their startled faces to starboard. The last thing they were to see was the broad orange bow of a Jersey registered trawler.

It was quite normal for the larger fishing boats to be at sea for ten days or more at a time but the smaller vessels were normally back within twenty four hours. They could stay away for a few days if they wished, by calling at other ports, but when they intended doing this their skippers would leave a note to that effect with their home fishing agents. That would ensure that any messages could get to the men, even when they were ashore elsewhere. If the decision to stay out was made while they were at sea or some circumstance was likely to delay their normal or intended return then these agents could be informed directly by marine radio.

None of these normal contingencies had been met by the skipper of the Beacon Belle. It was not like Fergus.

Murray MacPhail sat in the fishing agents' office on the pier tapping his pencil on the desk. He was a tall, slim man with gaunt features. Possessed of nervous energy, he would be the first to accept that he was a worrier. With him each unresolved matter immediately became a crisis and he was a magpie for unresolved matter.

Most of the small boats were back and a couple of the larger ones had also come in. The fishing agent was instinctively alert to overdue vessels in the way that an experienced shepherd might know, without counting, that his flock was incomplete.

He had asked one or two of the returning skippers if they had seen the Beacon Belle. They had offered no news but they had reassured Murray that Fergus would be all right. He was one of the best, they had reminded him, and not a man to take lightly the well-being of his young crew. Besides, the sea had been kindly and the weather had presented no threat.

Murray could accept every compliment of Fergus Morrison. He had come to know at first hand the quality of the man. Incomer or not, inland lowlander or not, Morrison had taken to fishing these coastal waters like a man finding his vocation in spite of himself.

With the arrival of nightfall Murray was quite uneasy. Never had he known Fergus to be this careless. Using the office VHF set he called the Beacon Belle. No response.

He glanced up at the notice board and saw the neatly printed intimation from Fergus, "THURSDAY OVERNIGHT WEST OF MULL. BACK TEATIME FRIDAY."

Murray lifted the telephone and dialled. The Coastguard officer listened with interest to Murray's misgivings.

He put out a general call for any fishing boat to report a Friday sighting of the Beacon Belle. None did. This was followed by telephone enquiries to the pier master offices within sailing distance of Fergus Morrison's beat. None had seen him. The Beacon Belle was missing.

Over the weekend police officers called at the homes of Jamie Cameron and Roddy McCuish. Their parents had heard nothing from them. The boys had been expected home on Friday or perhaps Saturday morning if they had gone for a drink and stayed overnight with friends. They had often done this but when the Beacon Belle had not berthed it was unlikely to be a possibility on this occasion.

Fergus Morrison's flat was locked up and his elderly neighbour was certain that Fergus had not returned. He never came home without checking on the old man and occasionally delivering him some fish.

The weekend brought no news and at first light on Monday the search began. Coastguard, police and civilian volunteers formed search parties, each with responsibility for a length of the Mull coastline. At sea the fishing fleet combined their daily business with a sea search, reporting their area of search and their lack of success.

Visibility was good and the Royal Navy agreed to provide a helicopter to sweep the area during daylight hours. It was never suggested to the Navy that they had a moral responsibility to be doing something. The sudden and unexplained disappearance of a small fishing boat had fuelled speculation. Even the moderate minded were giving an ear to the hasty and erroneous conclusions of the submarine suspecting skippers.

No accusation could or should be made in the absence of proof and the Coastguard had enquired politely of the Royal Navy and the U.S. Navy based on the Holy Loch as to the possibility of submarine involvement in the fate of the Beacon Belle. While the capability of a submarine to pull down a fishing vessel by her nets was accepted by both navies they denied having had any submarine in the area at the material time.

Among the fishermen the submarine remained the chief suspect. They remained cynical of official denials. Murray MacPhail was not cynical of the Royal Naval denials but he was uneasy. No submarine could pull down a boat by set lines and Fergus had gone after dogfish by set line.

The shore parties on Mull had found nothing that could be identified positively as having come from the Beacon Belle. Some had remarked on the inordinate number of wooden fish boxes in good condition they had found on the western foreshore of the island. Others expressed no real surprise at this. The fishing fleet recovered two marker buoys with flags and a single lifebelt. Some were certain that the gear belonged to the Beacon Belle and close inspection of the items revealed faded traces of the boat's registration.

Word got around and the local and national papers carried a formal statement. Over a week had passed and the parents of the young crewmen were beginning to accept what others had already accepted. Their boys were dead.

Fergus had no known relatives. Murray MacPhail had told this to the police but they broke into his flat just the same. They checked at the dental and medical clinics, the bank and the post office. Nowhere was it suggested that Fergus had any next-of-kin.

Among mariners, professional and amateur, speculation now began as to where and when the bodies of the fishermen would appear. The Coastguard computer could demonstrate tide and current movement so as to recommend possible locations but the information required for confident prediction was not available in the case of the Beacon Belle. It was generally agreed that the current patterns were unpredictable and the bodies could turn up anywhere and at any time. Equally, they might never show up. All police officers with island or coastal beats were instructed to pay vigilant attention to their shoreline for the arrival of any body or debris related to the tragic loss of the fishing boat. All other efforts were brought to a close.

Constable John Grierson was the local police officer to a large section of the hill farming community but his area also included the island of Orsaig. The island had a dozen or so farming families but those below retirement age had a day job on the mainland.

It had been some time since John Grierson had found any reason to visit the peaceable island. Nothing much ever happened on Orsaig and with no real roads to speak of, the prospect of walking around it never got to be a priority. The current instruction gave the tall officer the necessary encouragement to find the time and make the effort. He chose a sunny day and took the early ferry. The ferryman operated a passenger only service. Large freight required a specially chartered boat or raft.

A long walk over wild and rough terrain in the west highlands has the irony of being a ponderous prospect but a pleasant privilege. As John Grierson set out around the coastal perimeter he warmed to the task. Some day he would stop smoking he promised himself. He should throw himself out into the fresh air and sea breeze more often, no doubt about it. Working his way over the machair and the rocks he had no desire for a cigarette. Pity he could not spend every day this way.

His progress surprised him. By lunchtime he had completed almost three-quarters of the island's coast. He was now approaching the south-west corner of Orsaig and he had not halted from the outset. Climbing up a gully to avoid an inaccessible area of crag, Grierson suddenly found himself at the side of a white painted cottage. It was not a farm, even though domestic fowl ran about it, but a rented cottage in poor condition.

The cottage faced south and in front of the house a young woman sat in the sunshine singing softly to herself. As Grierson walked closer to her he could see that she was doing some embroidery work. It was almost inevitable that he should startle her. She was not expecting a visitor and certainly not one from the direction of the gully.

"Oh, you did give me a fright." she said, placing her hand on her chest and staring at him.

"Sorry." Grierson said formally. "I never saw you at first. No need to be afraid I can assure you. I am a police officer who visits the island from time to time."

She looked him up and down and took in the dark serge trousers and white, pocketed shirt with provision for epaulettes.

"You don't have all your uniform, do you?" she asked, smiling.

"On a day like this? I am walking round the island and I'm hot enough the way I am." he countered. He was trying to be pleasant, trying to accept the English accent which identified her as yet another white settler.

"Are you here on holiday or have you rented the cottage as a home?" he continued.

"Oh, it's our home." she replied, a little defensively.

"OUR home?" he repeated.

"Yes. I have a husband. He's a fisherman. He's out in his boat right now." "Maybe I'll meet him the next time I come over." Grierson said casually, turning to leave.

"Are you over a lot?" she asked hurriedly, as if she must have his answer before he left.

Grierson turned and shook his head. He blew out his cheeks and pulled his sticky shirt out from his body.

"You must be joking," he said with a laugh, "I might come back next year."

She shared the joke but there was a hint of relief in her laughter. "Be seeing you." Grierson shouted as he headed off.

"Goodbye." she said politely.

He kept the vision of her in his mind as he picked his way along the top of the rocks. She was healthy and attractive in appearance yet she was beginning to let herself go. Her hair showed the set and style of past care but was becoming a little loose, a little dirty and a little untidy. Her clothing was old fashioned, once trendy and of good quality, but the sort of laundering it required was unlikely to be found in that old cottage.

To Grierson she had looked like a girl of some breeding, unfortunate enough to be marooned on a deserted island. But Orsaig was not deserted and other women on the island had some care for their own appearance. This young lady had chosen her declining standards in deliberate rebellion against recognised values. John Grierson had been a police officer long enough to know a hippy when he saw one.

As he reached the top of the southern bluff he looked back at the cottage. He felt that he should know that house.

"Of course, it's Flashmore." he reminded himself.

He sat down on the heather and leaned back on the warmth of a dry mound of exposed rock.

It was some years now since the Customs men had chased the floating bales of grassy cannabis towards the shores of Orsaig. The discovery of the drug had sent a dozen or so people scurrying off to pastures new. One of them had been a man who had stayed there at Flashmore. What was that chap's name?

As he racked his memory for answers he reached into his pocket and took out his cigarettes.

The Parish Church filled slowly at first. The older skippers, most accompanied by their crew, nodded towards the local councillors and fishery officials. They had attended many funerals in their time and some had previously attended memorial services like this one. The absence of the coffins for those the sea had claimed was not a new phenomenon.

As the appointed time of eleven-thirty approached, the trickle of mourners became more of a stream. The young fishermen and their girlfriends did not arrive early at the church, nor did they dress with the same reverence as the older men and their breath gave the rear of the church an atmosphere which betrayed their previous gathering point. The nervous chattering and fidgeting reflected their discomfort and unfamiliarity with the solemn silence of the place.

Ahead of them on the forward pews were people from every walk of life. The schoolteachers who had taught both Roddy and Jamie, the dentist who had attended to their teeth since they first had teeth to be tended, the bank manager who had assisted and advised Fergus, the insurance man who had maintained a security over the Beacon Belle and the midwife who had delivered Jamie Cameron twenty four years earlier. These were the sort of friends who attended all funerals in the west highlands where men and women had not simply been members of the public, they had been part of the community. Tommy the barber looked sideways at the pew opposite. There he saw members of the shinty team Roddy McCuish had played for since leaving school. Tommy knew them all. Murray MacPhail sat with Donnie MacIntosh. Jamie and Roddy had always referred to him as "Diesel Donnie" for virtually every local fishing vessel took its fuel from Donnie MacIntosh. Young women who had been with the boys through school and more recently had spent time with them at local discotheques began to succumb to the sadness of the occasion.

Loretta MacAuley had known both boys since primary school. Her boyfriend, David Russell, had been Jamie Cameron's best friend all through school. Davy sat next to her, his head bowed.

The minister spoke out with a clear voice and a positive message. Spreading his arms towards the grieving relatives in the front pews he spoke of the loss they felt and the depth of love he had sensed when comforting them in their loss. He paid tribute to the contribution the young men had made to their community and their families.

He remarked on Fergus Morrison whose origins were uncertain but whose years in the west highland community had earned the respect and admiration of all who had come to know him.

The congregation rose to sing "Abide with me" and Loretta MacAuley looked around the sea of faces. She recognised them all to a greater or lesser extent until her gaze fell on a man standing in a pew occupied only by him.

He was mature and attractive and a stranger. Loretta was certain that the man did not belong to the local community and his being alone in a pew seemed to confirm this. She continued to watch him as he sang with some conviction, his attention visiting no one but the clergyman.

The minister prayed and gave thanks for the lives of the fishermen. He entrusted their souls to Almighty God and asked the congregation to keep their memory alive in their hearts.

As the pews emptied and Loretta followed Davy into the aisle she looked again at the stranger. He remained in his seat with his head slightly bowed, dwelling on his private thoughts. He obviously felt a sense of loss, but for whom? With his conservative grey suit and his well-groomed short hair he was unlike any fisherman. If he was related to Roddy or Jamie she would expect to know him. He looked to be about the same age as Fergus but Fergus had no relatives, even the minister had said so. Anyway, this man looked nothing like Fergus.

A gentle push from behind encouraged Loretta to move on down the aisle and leave the stranger to his meditation.

# TWO

"Do you think we are making any headway?"

Mary Fleming paused to look round the pile of unpacked boxes and considered her husband's question.

"Not much," she sighed, "but this is the price we have to pay for moving such a distance. Apart from washing the place out last weekend we have been able to do nothing in preparation for moving in. When we arrived with the furniture van the place was completely bare, no curtains up and no carpets down. At least we've made a start."

"We must get all of these boxes out of the front room before I can begin to think about laying the lounge carpet. Still, at least it's here and it's paid for." her husband remarked, nodding towards the large roll of good quality carpet that lay against the longest wall of the room. "I might be better to employ a carpet fitter for that job. I don't trust myself the same with these bigger carpets."

Mary looked at him and wondered if that was the real reason. He had managed well enough with the bedrooms and the hall. Perhaps he was just becoming fed up with laying carpets.

"We don't need any carpet fitter yet," she reminded him, "not to empty boxes."

They carried another two boxes to the bedroom. Outside, the children were running excitedly around the house. The workmen had left several odds and ends behind them when they had finished the house, enough for the children to continue "house building".

"I hope they stay near the door." Mary remarked each time the young voices fell silent. She knew that the garden had no boundary fences and must have appeared to the children to extend as far as the woods and the hill. It was only a matter of time before their curiosity took them off to explore.

"You'll have to let them play where they want to." her husband advised. "This place is a haven for children and a safe haven at that."

"I will feel a little easier in my mind when they are at school and more people know who we are." Mary said positively.

"At least we don't have to worry about them running out onto a busy road. Are there other children here for them to play with?" her husband asked, cutting the string from another cardboard box.

"Yes. The house up the road has young children. You know, where the doctor stays?" Mary replied. "Remember he waved to you from the red car when he was going home last night?"

"I remember. That's another thing about this place. Everyone waves to you as if they already know who you are. Have you noticed that?"

"I didn't expect the postman to ever find us." Mary said with a laugh. "Not only did he know who we are and where we stayed but he knew where we came from and what you worked at."

Her husband laughed.

"I bet he won't put off time in telling everyone else." he remarked. "I think it would be hard to keep secrets in this part of the world."

"Do you think we have done the right thing, Andrew?" she asked, looking directly at him.

"It is a bit early to be sure but I think we have. Ask me again when we have settled in. I must go in to meet my new boss and let him know that I have arrived. We haven't really seen anything except this house. What do you think of it?"

"It's lovely." Mary declared sincerely. "It is big and we will be stretched for a while trying to pay this new mortgage. You better ask this new boss of yours for some overtime."

Her husband smiled.

"I'm not sure what kind of an impression that would make." he replied. "Anyway, it's here at home that the overtime is needed if we are ever to get back to normal living again."

"Living here will be different." Mary said dreamily, turning her face towards the window. "It's so quiet at night and during the day the view is beautiful from that kitchen window."

"There must be places to walk to and places to take the kids on picnics. Did you notice the wee church? The children will pass it every day on their way to school."

"We should get back into the habit of going to church every Sunday." Mary said, sounding more like her positive self again. "If we cannot find the desire to attend church in these heavenly surroundings then I doubt that we ever would. Just think of it as part of the children's education and upbringing Andrew."

"I don't really have to be sold the idea. I agree with you. It will be interesting to see how little of a fashion parade the local congregation put on."

"So you'll come." said Mary with obvious delight. She had wanted them to attend as a family. "I need a break from this unpacking. After tea we should take a walk along the shore. We won't have the same opportunity once the children start school and you are back on these shifts."

"All right." her husband agreed. "Look for the box with the wellington boots."

"So you're Andrew Fleming."

THE WEED KILLER

Chief Inspector Stewart MacKellar smiled as he ushered the smartly dressed, newly arrived member of staff into his room. He pushed the door closed and indicated a seat.

"Sit down and tell me a bit about yourself. Usually the men we get coming to Corran Bay nowadays have nothing to tell. I get all the new recruits with no experience and I am supposed to pretend that I have all the manpower that I need. Just figures on paper, you understand? It makes a change to have someone with some service like yourself."

The Chief Inspector sat down and allowed the constable to take up the conversation.

"I have sixteen years service behind me and before that I was two years on a building site." Fleming announced.

"Did you have a trade?" asked the senior officer. "I was once a plumber you know. The man who taught me still has a business in this town."

"No, I had no trade." Fleming replied. "I should have gone to college but I decided that I had seen enough of study and I was conscious of my dependence on my parents. To be perfectly honest I didn't know what I wanted to do. I took a labouring job on a building site until I decided to join the police."

"You would realise a difference when you joined the police?" the Chief Inspector commented, inferring that improvement had been the difference.

"Yes, I certainly did." agreed Fleming. "All of a sudden I was working for half the money."

The Chief Inspector laughed.

"I seem to remember losing a few bob myself. Thankfully things have improved since these days and you wouldn't care to be throwing bricks about now, would you?"

"Probably not," Fleming conceded, "but the experience of the building site did me no harm, in fact it has been a benefit to me since I joined the police. It helped me to understand the principles applying to working class life and the areas I have worked in were full of working class people. I spent much of my time in sprawling housing schemes full of large families and with a high percentage of unemployed. They stole from one another and they gave to one another, they knifed one another and they nursed one another, they had rules for living but these did not always coincide with the law. The police tended to become a part of their lives and there could be understanding even when there was no agreement. Watching and understanding people has been a basic instinct in my work. The better I got to know them the better I could operate."

"You enjoyed working in a high crime rate area then?" asked the Chief Inspector in the pleasing lilt of his native soil. Around the walls of his room Fleming could see photographs, plaques and other mementoes of county days when most police careers were spent among ones home community. Particularly in areas such as the highlands the intrusion of regional authority was tolerated rather than welcomed.

"Aye. I got results and for me that was always rewarding." the constable replied evenly.

"You must obviously realise that you won't find the same high crime rate up here. Why did you choose to leave this satisfactorily busy area you were in to come to what I would like to think of as a more peaceful and law abiding environment? I understand that this transfer was due in some part to your own decision." the local police chief enquired with genuine interest.

"I have to consider my family and whether or not I want them to grow up in an area where the crime rate in any one street might be higher than you have here. They are just beginning school and my wife and I have made a conscious decision to put them first and give them the opportunity to grow up in fresh air and beautiful countryside. Some would say that I am opting out of the rat race but I honestly believe that in this part of the world my children can receive a good education and a sense of values, moral fibre and community spirit of the sort which regrettably no longer seems possible in overcrowded schools and a society too cautious to be kind." explained the constable with an easy delivery.

The Chief Inspector was beginning to warm to this man. Constable Fleming's previous boss had inserted a notation in the transfer papers expressing his surprise that such a talented police officer should choose to move to such a quiet and remote area. The inference was that a self-motivated man might not settle if work was scarce.

"I can understand a man who puts his family first," the Chief Inspector said softly, having found the notation slightly offensive, "but you must not feel that we have nothing to do here. Our work is of a different type and our problems are not with crime normally, but we do have our share of unpleasant work. This year so far we have employed a local undertaker no fewer than twenty six times. The deaths have come from road accidents, sailing and diving accidents, climbing accidents, exposure to the weather, suicides and the sudden but natural death of some visitors. It would appear that the natural beauty of the area attracts people whose end is near."

"The closer to heaven the shorter the journey." interjected the constable with a smile.

"Exactly so," confirmed the Chief Inspector, "but we don't always recover the bodies you know. A couple of months back we lost three local men on a fishing boat. They haven't turned up and neither has their boat. The boat must have gone down quickly, they never got out a 'mayday'."

"What would cause a thing like that?" asked the constable.

"In calm waters," the Chief Inspector said softly, remembering the weather conditions which had made the loss so inexplicable. He pressed the points of his fingers together in front of his substantial stomach and continued. "There can be few explanations. The favourite speculation among the fishermen is the possibility of a submarine pulling her down by her nets. The Navy have denied the presence of any submarine in the area. There is no real evidence for that theory, just the lack of good alternatives and the background of stories the fishermen tell in support of the idea. They have their suspicion but we have no facts and we may never know the truth of what happened to the 'Beacon Belle'". He widened his eyes and threw his hands apart as if to deliver an open verdict on the matter.

"So you found nothing suspicious about the disappearance of a fishing boat and three men?" Fleming asked quietly.

"We never found anything, suspicious or not" the Chief Inspector replied, bringing his hands together again. He did not need to be reminded by some newly arrived constable that the disappearance of the fishing boat was unresolved. The matter had been raised often enough by local folk. His room window overlooked most of the town and with a nod in that direction he continued, but changed the subject.

"Our town is a port and is very popular with tourists. The population trebles in the summer months and we have to cater for the additional traffic and scrutinise the licensed premises. All of which might sound a bit mundane to someone like yourself but these matters have to be addressed just the same."

At this point the Chief Inspector rose from his seat, indicating that the interview was almost over. He offered his hand once more.

"You will find life different here but I hope that you and your family will come to like staying here and settle down happily. If you ever need any help or advice with anything at all do not hesitate to knock this door. I am sure you will be an asset to our resources here."

Constable Fleming enjoyed listening to this new boss. He was someone who had grown up in this idyllic area when there had been less of an influence from the encroaching tentacles of the modern world.

Mary Fleming had been working since the minute her husband had left to see his boss. The children were constantly eager to help her but their excitement seemed to upset their best efforts.

When her husband came home she made coffee and told him that the builders' foreman had called to take a note of the various small faults they had noticed since moving into the new home.

"He is sending a man round to sort them out." she reported in a tired but contented tone.

She brought her husband up to date on the things she had learned from the few neighbours she had met until her stories were interrupted by a knock at the door. Andrew Fleming opened the door to a man in his late twenties.

"Hello. I'm the joiner. I've come to sort out the problems you told the foreman about."

As he worked, the joiner explained that he was only employed by the builders for specific tasks. His employment was not constant and was therefore neither secure nor well paid.

"What do you do yourself?" he asked of Andrew Fleming. Constable Fleming told him.

"Aw well. At least your job is secure." he replied graciously.

The joiner continued in pleasant conversation until all the minor faults had been attended to. Andy Fleming watched the man return to a faded Ford Cortina which sat at the kerb with the driver's door window rolled down and the keys in the ignition switch. The Chief Inspector had told him that life was very different here and Andy smiled as he remembered.

The weekend had allowed for most of the settling in work at home and Monday morning would see the children start at their new school.

"The children are so excited. I doubt if they will sleep at night." Mary told her husband.

"I just hope that I don't sleep either." commented Andy, due to begin nightshift on that same Monday.

He did not sleep, though the first few nights were quiet. The streets were also quiet as winter was approaching. Many of Fleming's new colleagues were like the Chief Inspector, native to the west highlands and Western Isles. They were part of the way of life around them and shared the interest that everyone seemed to have in everyone else's affairs.

Hamish MacLeod was typical. He had become amused by the broad honesty of this new constable from the lowlands. As they patrolled the centre of town together they were able to provide each other with cause for amusement.

By Thursday night the night life had become a little busier. In the cool evening air people shuttled to and from one licensed establishment or another, some stopping to commiserate with the on-duty Hamish.

Andrew Fleming had taken particular interest in two men walking just ahead of him. Both were dressed in denims. One was dark skinned and wore a red headband. As this pair reached the junction of a narrow side street the darker man tapped the other on the elbow and headed into the side street. His friend followed him.

As the police officers reached the junction they saw the two men turn from the side street into an alley. Nodding to Hamish MacLeod, Andy Fleming headed for the alley.

As they walked into the alley the police officers saw both men huddled together some fifteen feet away.

Immediately they became aware of the police presence the two men jumped apart. Their clothing was intact and only their reaction to the arrival of the police gave cause to believe that they were behaving improperly. Appearing to regain their composure, they began to walk towards the police officers and were stopped by Andy Fleming.

"So what attracted you two boys to this back street then?" he asked in a routine sort of way.

The coloured gent spoke out.

"Just meaning to soak the ground, man. Didn't mean no harm. You know there are no toilets around."

There was nothing west highland about this chap. A strong London accent giving a plausible answer which did not fit with what the officers had seen.

"Lucky for you we arrived so soon. Who are you anyway?"

"I am Benjamin Kasis and this here is Malky Masters." The dark man was still spokesman.

"Do you live here?" Andy Fleming asked Kasis.

"I moved here just a few months ago. I got a job on the Fernshaw Estate just south of town. I rent one of the estate cottages. Gardenin' that's my scene, man."

"And what about you Mr. Masters?"

"I stay in Island Terrace. I don't have a job." replied Malky, his voice soft and mannerly, his accent lowland Scots.

"Okay lads. On your way. You'll find a toilet in any bar."

Both men left quickly without a further word and neither looked back.

"They never came round here to pee." said Hamish trying to show some streetwise sense to a man who had known nothing else.

"No. You're right." acknowledged Andy Fleming who had begun to search the ground around where the man had been standing.

"The ground's dry." offered Hamish.

Andy did not answer but kept searching until his eye caught a small ball of clear film. He picked it up and began to unwrap it. He removed something similar to a small beef stock cube from the film and put it in his pocket.

"What's that?" asked Hamish.

"They call it hash, marijuana or leb. I call it cannabis resin but whatever you want to call it, just having it in your possession is an offence."

"Dope." said Hamish. "I've heard the boys talking about it but I have never seen it before."

Andy had taken a small penknife from his pocket and approached a curl of dog dirt hardening at the side of the alley. Cutting off the point of it he then placed the hard point in the cling film and wrapped it up. He put this package back where he had found the piece of cannabis.

"Let them smoke that." he told Hamish, who had already begun to giggle.

"Do you suppose there's much dope about here?" Fleming asked Hamish. "It was becoming quite common down where I was working before I came here. Even the youngest of kids were into it."

"Just a few years ago an organised gang tried to bring a ton of it ashore from a boat. Most of them were caught and a lot of cannabis was lost in the sea." Hamish reported, trying to sound well informed, but he was also quick to point out that the events of which he spoke had occurred before his time.

"That sort of amount wouldn't be for the locals to use. I just bet that few of the organised gang were people who actually belonged here." Andy offered for Hamish to respond.

"No. Some of them had been in the area for quite some time beforehand right enough but none of the ringleaders had been brought up here. Big John Grierson will tell you better about it. He was here then and Orsaig is part of his beat. That's where the stuff was to come ashore, that island over there." Hamish said, simply nodding his head towards the sea for at night Orsaig could not be seen in the darkness.

A few nights later Andy found John Grierson alone in the office canteen.

"You're quite right. They were all incomers." Grierson confirmed. Constable John Grierson had similar service to Andy Fleming and was credited with a great deal of common sense. He was a third generation police officer and never someone with too much to say. As a good policeman being underworked in a quiet area he had found the cannabis incident on Orsaig an immensely fascinating experience. Since his most recent visit to the island he had spent some time reminiscing and now had no difficulty in recalling almost every detail. Even so he was not prepared to allow his enthusiasm for the subject to turn his normal reticence into flowing divulgence. He would not normally furnish replies to people whose sole purpose for asking was idle curiosity. He sensed that Andy Fleming's interest was professional but he did not wish to discuss the matter beyond the questions raised.

"I would guess that they came from the south coast of England, either somewhere in Devon or some of the larger ports." Andy suggested, aware that he had not yet gained the complete confidence of his colleague. He knew that while his interest and intellect was being examined he would have to content himself with Constable Grierson's slow and reluctant response. Other new colleagues had advised him that while the surrounding sea lochs were deep, none were as deep as this man.

# THE WEED KILLER

John Grierson looked back at him through the smoke of a cigarette held close to his mouth. His expression was one of studious staring.

"They were nearly all from the south of England and some stayed on Orsaig for months before the incident. The ringleader stayed at Flashmore Cottage on the west of the island."

"If that is so," continued Andy thoughtfully, "could they not have been importing the stuff successfully during these months?"

"The Customs boys didn't think so. They reckon that all the planning was done over these months in readiness for one big shipload."

"And what do you think?" asked Andy, skilfully suggesting a personal trust in the big fellow's opinion.

"You could be right." Grierson said evenly.

"Could that same activity have started up again?" Andy pressed.

"Perhaps." replied Grierson.

"Are you not sure?" asked Andy in something nearing reproach.

"You're quite right." big John said firmly, rising to his feet and crushing out his cigarette. "I'm not sure."

He turned and left. For the time being, their conversation was over.

The weeks passed and Andy was now more at ease with his new surroundings. The swooping, screaming seagulls no longer brought laxative surprise and the smell of the harbour was less of a stink. Indeed, now that he was working daylight hours he visited the pier daily and showed a constant interest in the fishing boats.

The fishermen formed a very close-knit fraternity but a few of them had taken to cautious nodding or even waving to the new policeman.

Andy Fleming realised that the locals had a natural curiosity of him which they would seek to satisfy by quizzing anyone they saw as a link between him and them. It was therefore quite intentional that Andy was to be seen in frequent conversation with the pier master, Norman MacDougall. Norman was an official but not so much of an official as to be aloof of the fisherman.

Every word the police officer spoke to the pier master was designed to portray a lowland, inland man with no knowledge of, but great interest in, all things to do with boats and the sea. The interest of an innocent newcomer and not the prying eyes and ears of the nosy official. That was the picture.

It seemed to be working for in time the nods and waves became more frequent and relaxed. Through the pier master Andy was gaining the confidence of the fishermen and his presence on the pier was no longer a matter of any apprehension.

Donald MacIntosh was another man with a sound overall knowledge of the fishing fleet. He seemed to provide every boat with its fuel and Andy Fleming had not been slow to appreciate the value of such a man.

As the two men spoke together one day in the sunshine about the plans to alter the pier, a white hulled craft roared into the harbour with its bow in the air. As the throttle was pulled back and the vessel fell forward off the plane it became an obvious topic of conversation.

"Now there goes a man of mystery." remarked Donnie MacIntosh in his soft highland tones. "Do you know that that boat has a 230 horsepower engine? She can do over twenty knots and with that crazy bugger at the wheel she is going at that sort of speed for most of the time."

"That must be very heavy on fuel." observed Andy, hoping to prompt some facts and figures from Donnie.

"It must be," agreed Donnie, "but don't ask me how much. He orders his fuel through the franchise garage in town. I'll tell you this though, the man is the talk of the place with his fancy new boat and its big engine. They say he is fishing the shellfish for the French market but he will have to catch one hell of a lot of shellfish before that boat and engine will pay for itself. It's all kitted out with the best of radar and satellite navigation too."

By this time the craft had reached the pier and was being tied up by the fisherman, a particularly scruffy individual.

"He doesn't look like he has two pennies to rub together." Andy commented. "Do you know his name?"

"No, as a matter of fact, I do not." Donnie replied with a note of amazement at his own ignorance.

"Where could I get it?" asked Andy.

"I dare say the Fisheries Officer should have it. The boat should be registered with him." Donnie replied slowly, the police officer's interest having scarcely escaped him.

Andy Fleming realised this and in order to dampen any stimulation of Donnie's imagination he went on to explain.

"If this guy's fishing is not viable he might not meet his fuel bills at the garage and there might be complaints of fraud or something similar. I would want to know who he is beforehand and then I would be able to recognise the position."

"Oh. I see. I wouldn't be at all surprised if it turns out that way. Maybe it's just as well he didn't come to me for his fuel after all." Donnie said with a nod of his head, apparently accepting the false explanation.

As he walked past the tied up vessel Andy Fleming took a mental note of her name and registration.

On leaving the pier he noticed the scruffy fisherman at the back of a parked van. The driver of the van came round to join him and to open the back doors. Andy Fleming stopped momentarily. He recognised the van driver, it was Benjamin Kasis.

Kasis handed the fisherman a small gas cooker and a gas container which they carried to the boat.

A few minutes later and Constable Fleming was in front of the franchise garage and passing the time of day with the pump attendant when the son of the owner came out of the building and made for a parked Range Rover. Here was the very man who, according to the pump attendant, was responsible for all commercial fuel supply by the firm.

Several minutes' innocent conversation over the advantages of diesel to petrol in marine craft eventually led to the example provided by the police officer.

"That boat goes through a fortune in fuel every month. It runs to hundreds of pounds but the bills get paid just the same." remarked the garage accountant.

"Who pays them?" asked Andy with a laugh. "Rockefeller?"

"No." replied the garage man, accepting the humour. "It's actually some foreign guy from down south who owns the boat. He pays all the bills."

"These foreigners have all the money. Still, they must be good for business. Nice talking to you. See you again sometime."

Andy smiled as he half raised his hand in farewell. It was a mannerism which had become a characteristic habit of his over the years.

Even the bright sunshine could do nothing to brighten the brass plate on the sandstone wall but the words "Fishery Office" could still be read.

"Good afternoon. I think you are Mr. Little." Andy said cheerily as he stretched a hand out towards the young man behind the extremely old desk. "I am Constable Fleming."

"Billy Little." the young man replied softly, accepting the police officer's hand. "What can I do for you?"

"It may not be anything at all," Andy began, "but I have a small suspicion about a very scruffy fisherman with a very expensive boat. I wonder if you know enough about it to put my mind at ease."

"I can imagine who you are talking about." Billy Little said with a smile. "I have some papers on that boat. Just give me a minute."

He headed for a filing cabinet.

"Here we are. The boat is the "Hand Maiden", built a year ago. Registered down south nine months ago. She has been here for six months. The price was £37,000 plus VAT. She is a forty footer owned by the "Van Dongen Fishing Company". Mr. Claas Van Dongen resides in Portsmouth."

"Is the boat catching much fish?" asked the constable.

"Declared catches since she came here amount to £1,200."

"Considering the fuel she must use, do you consider her viable?" Andy asked cautiously.

"I very much doubt it." replied the Fishery Officer. "That guy who fishes her must be struggling to scrape a living."

"Have you got a name and address for him?" Andy enquired, pointing towards the open file on the desk.

Billy Little looked over the papers.

"Oh yes. Here we are. Harry Manson, Flashmore Cottage, Orsaig Island."

The village congregation of healthy proportions poured out into the Sunday morning sunshine.

Finally Fleming managed to winkle Mary and the children out of the small crowd and set them on the road home. The children ran on ahead.

"These people are all so friendly and unpretentious," said Mary. "They were almost queuing up to speak to me. I felt a wee bit like a celebrity yet they all approached me as if they had known me for years."

"I found the same thing." Andy Fleming agreed. "The men approached me as a group and the first of them was that doctor with the red car. He's a scientist you know, not a medical doctor. He introduced me to the others as if I should know them and the introductions were just a formality. He introduced one man as Buchanan from… and then he said some Gaelic name. He explained where that place was by naming the place next to it. I was completely lost but they didn't expect me to be, so I just nodded my head. Surely they realise that we are here only a couple of weeks and cannot be expected to know everyone and everywhere by now."

Her husband's voice showed some impatience and Mary laughed sympathetically.

"I was invited to join the W.R.I., 'the Rural' is what they call it. It meets in the church hall every Tuesday evening. Remember the minister mentioned it?" Something in her voice told Andy that his wife had already accepted the invitation.

"Oh yes, the minister. What do you make of him?" Andy Fleming asked with a chuckle. "He is a comical old man with a voice I could listen to all day. I fancy he thinks in Gaelic and speaks in English. Not everything comes out the way he intends it to."

"That just makes him all the more homely." Mary said easily.

"He spoke to me after we came out of the church and he told me that he had met the children."

"Yes, he has." Mary remembered. "They said that the minister had been in the school and had spoken to them. I meant to tell you that."

"Apparently he is due to retire soon." Andy said quietly. "Just a matter of his finding a house."

Having taken so readily to the old minister and then learning that he was about to retire seemed like good news and bad news at the same time and neither of them spoke again until they caught up to the children.

"This pair can start Sunday school next Sunday and one of the women was telling me that they can join the Cub Scouts and the Brownies."

Mary had said this loud enough for the children to hear and now she studied them for their response. They smiled. By now they knew that all local children were members of these groups and they had no wish to be different.

"Now," said Mary turning to her husband, "if you can unlock the door we can have some lunch."

"Go right on in." he replied with a wave of his hand. "It isn't locked."

The quiet months of winter allowed Andrew Fleming and his family to settle comfortably in their new environment. The weather at the coast was not as threatening as they had imagined while the benefits they had hoped for exceeded their expectations. The majestic scenery around them changed daily in daylight that could dazzle or dim and mists that would mould to a hillside before moving on. The children enjoyed small class numbers where everyone was a friend, including the teacher. As the old year became the new, the Flemings' home became a celebration station for the friends they had made and they wanted to belong. Mary would never again wonder if they had done the right thing.

With the coming of Easter weekend and the arrival of some warm weather, the town became more vibrant.

"Surely this place doesn't get any busier than it is tonight." Fleming remarked.

"It's certainly the busiest that I've seen it." Pearson informed him.

The two officers walked together along the esplanade towards the town centre. They had visited several of the hotel lounge bars and witnessed maximum crowds in each one. The street itself was busy as the more sober minded took a last stroll along the sea front before heading for a hotel or guest house bed.

They were more fortunate or more organised than some for the Tourist Office had reported as early as teatime that no more registered accommodation was available. The police office knew of some unregistered addresses and for a while had been able to find vacancies for late arrivals. By ten o'clock at night it had become impossible to find a single bed within a twenty five mile radius. Late arrivals were faced with the choice of sleeping in their vehicles or moving on.

The weather was mild and the police officers knew that later in the night, when licensed premises had spewed out their customers, young people would be found sleeping in all sorts of weird places.

In the meantime and until two in the morning the customers would continue to enjoy the sheltered comfort of lounge and disco bars.

Steve and Alan were from Port Glasgow and they had a tent pitched on the grassy area between the coast road and the sea about two miles out of town. Both were seventeen years of age and had left school the previous summer. They were not yet employed and their lack of money and years meant that they were unable to spend time in the licensed bars where the action was assumed to be. The two friends had been allowed to go on holiday together for the first time on condition that they behaved. Their impecunious state would scarcely allow them to do otherwise.

They did at least want to be near the activity and they found a public seat in the town centre. There they sat watching the world go by, finding much to amuse them as a large cross section of humanity passed before them demonstrating the annihilating effect of alcohol on personal inhibitions.

A bearded man in his late thirties sat down beside them and took the blue rucksack from his back.

Some eighty yards away Andy Fleming and Ian Pearson stopped at the road junction.

"Think we should stand here for a spell." suggested Fleming. "Give the legs a rest. We can see in three different directions from here."

"Look at the speed of these bloody taxis." remarked Pearson as a taxi sped past them, creating a breeze.

"I suppose they're a lot busier than usual." Fleming considered.

"No excuse." Pearson insisted.

Their attention was suddenly drawn to a commotion further down the street.

Stevie was shouting and screaming and viciously throwing his fists and feet about him at no-one in particular. He seemed to be totally oblivious to those who were there and his lifelong friend Alan was now apparently someone he could fail to recognise. Alan threw his arms around Stevie and called out to him to calm down but his friend acted as though in some form of fit and developed a strength well beyond his normal. Turning his body with great force Stevie threw Alan aside and, still screaming, ran mindlessly into the roadway.

While the attention of every pedestrian in the street was on Stevie, the attention of a fast moving taxi driver was not and the unfortunate driver received no warning as the young man ran directly into his path.

As young Alan rose from the footpath he saw his friend tossed into the air. The sudden cessation of the screaming served to emphasise the quietness of the moment as the young body, so highly charged with energy a moment before, turned slowly over the taxi like a stringless puppet before falling to the road surface with no sound and no movement.

Alan screamed and ran to his friend.

Fleming and Pearson ran towards the fallen man, Fleming calling on his radio for an ambulance to be summoned immediately.

The taxi had screeched to a halt and the driver now emerged from behind a shattered windshield and a

"Did he put anything in it apart from tobacco?" Fleming persisted.

"I wasn't watching the whole time. I did see him with a small plastic container like you would get a film in, you know, for a camera. I don't know what he had in it or what he did with it. The cigarette looked normal but the man did say that it was 'special'." Alan remembered.

"Did you smoke it at all?" Fleming asked him.

"I don't smoke. I had a wee puff because the man kept pestering me. It was awful. I was nearly sick. Steve kept smoking it. He has been smoking for nearly six months now. His mother would kill him if she...."

He sank his face in his hands and sobbed.

"Was that man there when Stevie started acting funny?" Fleming asked quietly.

"No. He had left by then." Alan replied without lifting his head.

"I don't suppose he told you who he was?" Fleming continued.

"No."

"Then I want you to tell me what he looked like."

The next few hours were spent interviewing the taxi driver and witnesses before completing the road accident report. By the time Fleming and Pearson were able to resume their patrol of the street daylight had returned and the place seemed empty of all but the seagulls. They had been scavenging the litter bins and strutted from one piece of paper to another seeking greasy morsels. Whenever one seemed to find something others would fly at it in jealousy. Both sides squawked and squealed continually and the street could not have been described as quiet.

The police officers met the usual early risers. The milkman, the cleaning lady, the man who opens the newsagents shop and the bakery delivery driver. Every so often the officers would come across a family sleeping in their car or some student type, too late for the hostel, sleeping in a doorway.

The night was almost over when the tired eyes of Constable Pearson spotted a brown hiking boot protruding from the open vestibule of the parish church.

The owner of the boot was lying across the floor of the vestibule, partly covered by a sleeping bag. Beside him lay a rucksack.

"Wake up." said Pearson coarsely, kicking the protruding leg.

The sleeping man stirred and then turned to face the officers. He was thirty-odd and bearded. The officers looked at each other.

The man gave his name and address as required and informed the police that he was a schoolteacher at a secondary school in the Glasgow area.

Andy Fleming informed him that he had reason to believe that a man answering his description had provided a controlled drug to a young man earlier in the night. The man agreed to being searched and the officers began a systematic search of his person.

From the trouser pocket of the secondary school teacher Fleming drew out a plastic container of the type normally used in the protection of photographic film. He eased the lid from the container and sniffed the thick syrup-like contents. He passed it to Pearson so that he could do the same.

"Cannabis oil." declared Fleming. "Just the sort of thing to send an unaccustomed young man right out of his mind. It will have to be analysed of course but I am satisfied that this substance is a controlled drug within the meaning of the Misuse of Drugs Act 1971. That being so I suspect you of having supplied this drug to a young man in the early hours of today. Both that supply and your present possession of the drug are offences under the Act. In respect of both these offences I must caution you that you need not say anything in relation to the offences. If you choose to say something then any statement you make will be noted in writing and may be used in evidence. Do you understand?"

"I understand." the teacher replied quietly.

"Is there anything you wish to say?"

The teacher hung his head and shook it slowly. He said nothing. The full import of what he had done was not yet known to him but it was something he was beginning to sense.

Ian Pearson fidgeted with excitement as he scribbled out the report requesting analysis of the oil. With a solemn face Fleming watched him.

"Are you not just delighted that we got him?" Pearson asked, flashing a smile in Fleming's direction.

"In another hour or so the young chap's parents will be here to identify their son. If he was going to be alive when they arrived I would be delighted." Fleming took a deep breath and threw his head back before continuing. "The paperwork will say that a taxi killed him but you and I know that he was killed by the effect of cannabis oil, cannabis oil given to him by a man who might have been responsible for part of the boy's education until just over a year ago. Some teacher huh?"

Fleming wandered towards the door.

"I'm going for a coffee, want one?"

# THREE

"Shall we go through to the lounge for our coffee, Mr. Whelan? I can offer you a fine cigar if you wish."

"Certainly my friend. As a Dutchman you should know all about good cigars."

The two men rose from the table but paused to give proper place to the lady.

"Mrs. Van Dongen I must thank you for a truly exquisite meal." gurgled Whelan, placing his hand over his stomach in a manner of satisfaction.

"You are too kind Mr. Whelan." the lady responded as she stepped forward to lead the way to the lounge. "I must admit to preparing the menu only Mr. Whelan. I have an excellent cook who prepares the meals."

"Yes, dear fellow. You must compliment the team as they complement each other." observed Claas Van Dongen, ever eager to portray his understanding of English.

When the choice of coffee had also been complimented Miep Van Dongen left the men to their brandy and cigars.

"Your house is truly splendid, Claas." remarked Robert Whelan as he cast his gaze around the sumptuous fittings of the large lounge. He stared at the paintings and wondered if they were genuine Dutch originals but resisted the urge to enquire as this would only serve to disclose his lack of expertise. "I can only assume that you are not relying entirely on shellfish for this living."

The Dutchman laughed.

"There is a certain amount of profit to be made from a certain amount of loss. But you are the last person I need to tell that to, eh Robert?"

"That is true." agreed Whelan, joining in the laughter. "The fishing brought me plenty, even if the fish never did" He looked around the room again. "Flashmore was nothing like this mind you, but it did have a certain rustic charm. It was a healthy place for me and my bank account while it lasted."

He accepted a fat cigar from the box held out to him by Van Dongen.

"Was it all cannabis in these days?" the Dutchman asked, placing the flame of a marble table lighter close to his own cigar.

"Aye, it was. It came in all forms, but strictly cannabis." He reached for the lighter. "That is still the bread and butter of the business but coke and heroine are big earners, heroine especially."

"I suppose so." said the Dutchman as he watched Whelan draw on his cigar. "My own country is no stranger to any of it but I must say that I find the whole culture distasteful, extremely distasteful."

Whelan's eyes flashed through the cigar smoke.

"It is distasteful, Claas. It is also profitable, precisely because it is distasteful. Why do you suppose so many of us have devoted as much of our time to setting up the network? The profits far outweigh any thoughts of repugnance."

"How did the others make out?" asked Van Dongen.

"They have all done well. One is still up in Skye where he has bought his third consecutive fishing boat. One has a successful public house, another a car showroom and "Hippy Dan" is just putting the finishing touches to a modern mansion just outside Edinburgh. I don't know what they will make of him. He is still drawing unemployment benefit."

"And you bought a hotel." added Van Dongen. "How is the hotel doing?"

"I sold it last March. Didn't make much on the sale but then the place was needing a lot of work done."

"But the sale gave you enough to set up this new financial venture of yours." observed the Dutchman, bringing the conversation back to the point of the evening.

"I prefer to call it a capital investment enterprise." declared his guest, raising and spreading his arms in the manner of an elixir salesman. The Dutchman was obviously unimpressed by this approach. He had built a successful, legitimate business in the manufacture of microchips for the motor industry and was not the type to buy from an elixir salesman. Whelan dropped his hands and sobered his expression.

"Each participating company will originally invest in the others. Outside of that investment there will be no tangible connection between them. "Whelan resumed, lifting his glass of brandy, but pausing briefly to gather his thoughts on his presentation of the proposed scheme. He knew that Van Dongen would listen out of intrigue but would agree to nothing until his business judgement had been seduced.

"All right, Robert. You want money from me. I am still listening." the Dutchman prompted flatly.

"We make a lot of money." declared Whelan. "But paradoxically it comes from loss-making concerns. If this paradox is noticed, and it is open to the public eye, then we become suspect. Unexplained wealth is all too readily associated with drugs nowadays. I have even read of government plans to legislate for the confiscation of assets gained from drug trafficking. What I propose is to isolate the money from the drugs so that the participants like yourself can claim to be doing no more than investing money for long-term profit. It would mean that your profit was less immediate but no complicity could ever be inferred, far less proved, against you and your money would be safe from the results of any drug trafficking offences."

"How do you achieve this? What am I supposed to be investing in, after all, if not my co-conspirators?" Van Dongen argued.

"By putting into place a number of additional small businesses which are not designed to be loss-making. They will be viable retail outlets in the hands of people who have proved their competence in the drug trade by maintaining clean records and a healthy lifestyle. They have the capital to start up in business for themselves but their sudden show of wealth would have to be explained by loans provided by our financial enterprise scheme. They would then be seen to be repaying such loans or applying for further loans, all from a registered finance company, but basically the process would conceal the management of drugs money. The businesses could eventually settle back into respectability."

Whelan stopped to sip his brandy and deliberately avoided the gaze of Van Dongen. He knew that his host would now pose any questions he might have or simply deliberate on what had been said.

The Dutchman lowered his brandy glass to his thigh as he considered the benefits of such a scheme. He had a solid business reputation behind him and his greatest fear was the threat to his legitimate success posed by his adventurous dabbling into the menacing business of drugs. His business acumen was a matter of record and respect, but even his friends at the Rotary and Bridge Clubs had passed casual comments on his apparent ability to swim upstream against recessional tides. What Whelan had said of obvious paradoxes was ominously true and what use was profit if it had to be concealed? Financial investment in the hands of an independent company could well be the answer. How good was Whelan? It had been a promise from Whelan that had encouraged him to purchase the Hand Maiden for Manson. That promise had been kept when the outlay had been repaid within three months and had now been repaid ten times over. The money was still coming and that was the rub, how to explain such income in the face of his seemingly pointless funding of Manson.

"Who will give Manson the money he needs?" the Dutchman asked quietly.

"I think you must continue to pay the expenses of fuel, equipment and repairs to the boat, Claas. Any departure from present practices would create a link with the unspecified funding which would have to replace your own, *vis-a-vis*, drugs money. Manson himself can be paid directly in cash but you must be seen to be supporting the boat that you own. You can set it against tax, can you not? "

"How much investment do you want from me?" the Dutchman asked, sipping his brandy.

Whelan was prepared for the question.

"I have calculated from a base figure of one million in total." he replied firmly. "I know what you have gained so far and I reckon that another hundred grand on top of that would represent a fair share and decent investment."

Van Dongen said nothing but pursed his lips and frowned. The top-up figure was an unexpected gamble.

"I anticipate receiving no less from the others," Whelan argued, "myself included."

Claas Van Dongen rested his brandy glass on his thigh once more and cast his eyes towards a broadly brushed portrait by Frans Hals. Van Dongen had not progressed by gambling. On the other hand he had always believed, like his father before him, that an asset known to be appreciating was no gamble. The temptation was there, even if it was accompanied by a nagging doubt.

"Tell me Robert. If my money is going into investment companies set up by you, how do I know that you will not simply take my share of the money and run?"

Robert Whelan spent a brief moment feigning hurt and insult but he had already sensed his colleague's underlying co-operation. With a wry smile he replied.

"You have no cause to worry about your money Claas. I will have all the worry and don't think I won't pay myself well for living with it. That will be enough for me to think about without trying to rob my partners. The others would not be pleased if you were to withdraw your boat."

"Yes." said the Dutchman thoughtfully. "These other partners are people I do not know nor care to know but I am a little concerned about them knowing me."

"You have no real worry on that score either." Whelan reassured. "They could probably find out that you were a party to the scheme of things but when they asked you why you had pulled out what would you tell them? That I had made off with your money. They would think of their own money and come looking for me. No, you need not worry Claas. I am in the same position as you and them. I have money at stake here and the present risks are enough without putting my life on the line. You and I are gentle businessmen Claas, but some of them are hard-bitten haulage contractors and night club owners. They have muscle of their own and they know where to hire more. I would not dare to cross them."

"They do not sound like model citizens Robert. I have no desire to be in business with gangsters, no matter how remote the connection."

"These are not the reputable men of whom I spoke earlier Claas. These are the people at the hard work end of things in the drugs trade. Their boats, like yours, have a part to play. Their juggernaut lorries travel the length and breadth of the country with live shellfish. Their leisure outlets and clubs disperse the stuff and take in the money that we are all so pleased to receive. I have organised these people Claas. They could afford to cross me if only they knew it. The best way for me to keep ahead of the game is to offer some insurance and the opportunity to make the golden egg a little bigger. They deal in businesses where most payment is outwith their book-keeping. It is fairly simple to deal with these people in a fireproof fashion."

"So we remain respectable." Van Dongen said with a nod of his head. He would always be careful in his dealings with Whelan but he had accepted in principle to co-operate. "And how much will this capital investment enterprise bring us?"

"I have estimated that in the five years, if all goes well, the money involved will be in the order of twenty million pounds." Whelan reported, trying to sound confident but unexcited. "But making any estimation is difficult. It depends on everything remaining healthy within the set-up."

"That money sounds good but how much will it pay initially?" Van Dongen enquired.

"Initially, Claas, I would hope it would pay you nothing at all." Whelan said simply.

"Nothing!" exclaimed Van Dongen. "What would be the point of that?"

"The point of that is the same as with any trust fund. The first monies are needed to set up the organisation before any interest can start to return to the founders. What you have laid out so far has already been paid back. By that I mean the boat and the sundry expenses involved in keeping your shell fisherman in place. You haven't lost so far and I am not asking you to lose now. The money from the next few turns will provide a form of insurance for people like yourself and Cranston by putting in place an investment network. After that you will receive fortunes in clean money. Anyone trying to prove otherwise would be chasing their tail."

"Who is this Cranston?" asked Van Dongen.

"Someone who has a much greater stake in all this than yourself." Whelan said, tossing his head slightly to emphasise the significance of Cranston.

"And would he have access to my money?" Van Dongen quizzed.

"No, absolutely not, in fact he need not even know that your money is there. I will give you details shortly of where your money will be deposited and where it can be accessed in a few months' time. All I would ask of you in the meantime is that you remain patient and do not seek to withdraw anything for a month or two. I shall ensure that your cut from the next few shipments goes directly into the business I provide for it and of course you will be at liberty to consult me at any time if you have any misgivings. I have no intentions of running away, I assure you."

"Very well," said Van Dongen, finally raising his brandy glass, "I look forward to hearing from you. Here's to our first million."

The lounge door opened and Mrs. Van Dongen entered.

"Ah Miep my dear. Robert has been admiring your paintings. You are more of an expert than I am, perhaps you would care to enlighten him. The way he has been talking he may be in a position to invest in one of his own some day."

The thirty foot open deck launch drew in beside the jetty. The six men aboard were similarly dressed and they could easily have been taken for the crew of a fishing boat. The launch carried no equipment for fishing however and her large deck space was completely clear.

As the launch bumped against the stone steps a group of four men at the top of the steps came forward and accepted the fore and aft mooring ropes thrown to them from below. The narrow steps dictated that the six men leave the launch in single file but as the first of them reached the top step two of the group of four took hold of him by the arms. They led him off towards a Ford Sierra parked nearby.

The two men who had tied off the mooring ropes joined the five coming ashore from the launch and bombarded them with questions.

"How did it go?"

"Is he the only one?"

"Where's the gear?"

From the other side of the harbour a large figure in an expensive sheepskin jacket watched these men through powerful binoculars. Beside him stood a well-built but slightly smaller man who stared in the same direction, apparently with no need for binoculars.

"Yeah. The bastards have got Ricky all right. No sign of the stuff. He must have ditched it." the man with the binoculars announced.

"Think he'll talk?" the other man asked laconically.

"No, not Ricky, he's too damn smart. He knows what to say. Come on. Better get the books ready for the boys in blue."

He lowered his glasses and turned towards the car.

The Ford Sierra pulled in at the side of the small police office.

Ricky Walsh was by now handcuffed to both the men who had taken him into the car and had no alternative but to accompany them through the office doors, along a corridor and into a small interview room. After a careful note had been taken of his identification and he had been advised of his rights the room door was closed and he found himself in the company of two men.

"We have managed to recover most of what you threw overboard Mr. Walsh, so there can be no doubt about what we have here, a bit of importation under the Excise Management Act. We know the boat isn't yours, so whose is it?" asked the man who was obviously about to play the part of interrogator.

"I hired it." replied Walsh.

"Who from?"

"Cranston Shipping Company."

"Is that where you were taking the stuff?"

"No. They got nothin' to do with it."

The interrogation lasted for two hours but Walsh insisted against reason that he had been acting alone. The investigators had tried every approach they could think of with Walsh but he was obstinately silent. They eventually led him off to a cell.

Lying alone in the cell he chuckled to himself.

His interrogators had seemed to assume that he would have brought the baled cannabis ashore on Jersey. They had seen him leave with an empty boat and they had found him in a boat which carried brown watertight bales under a blue tarpaulin. They had hailed him to stop and they had seen him try to outrun them, ditching his cargo as he went. They had caught him but they had never seen anyone else and they had no idea where he had been heading. It had never occurred to these silly bastards that the bales were watertight for a reason. They had him, Ricky Walsh, heah sure, he had no hope of getting away with it. It would be safer for Walsh if he made no attempt to defend himself in court. He knew that and what was just as important, he had not harmed "Garth" Cranston. The shipments could continue to run as before. Nothing had happened to damage Cranston's organisation. It was just as watertight as these bales that Walsh could hear the men unloading at the rear of the police office.

Walsh almost laughed out loud as he imagined Jacques Troutam running around in circles at the rendezvous point, cursing loud and long in French at the absence of Walsh and "les paquets".

The two men in dark suits looked the house over as they approached it on foot. The large turning circle of coloured paving was empty but the outer storm doors were open and beyond the diamond cut glass of the inner door a small table lamp burned needlessly.

One of the men pressed the doorbell and they gave each other a disgusted look as they heard a less than orchestral rendition of "Land of Hope and Glory" from within. The reclining stone lions on either side of the doorsteps seemed equally unimpressed.

A heavily made up woman in her early thirties came to the door dressed in a multi-coloured kimono and sporting jewellery on all parts for which jewellery had ever been designed.

"Yes." she enquired with a hint of haughtiness.

"Good day. I am detective Constable Goodhew, Mrs. Cranston. This is Mr. Russell of Her Majesty's Customs. Is your husband at home?"

Mrs. Cranston performed a change of facial expression which threatened the adhesion of her make-up.

"No, he's not here. I can get him on the car 'phone. Is there any trouble?"

"Just a few questions on a matter we think he can help with." Colin Goodhew replied in a routine tone.

"Just a moment. I'll see where he is."

She skipped off in the direction of the kitchen, ignoring the telephone beside the shining light on the hall table. She returned a few minutes later.

"He's down town. He says he can meet you at his office if that suits you. Do you know where it is?"

Colin Goodhew assured her that he knew where the offices of Cranston Shipping Company were and thanked her for her help.

Trevor Gareth Cranston wore a huge smile as he came to meet the two enquiring officers. For them he would be Mr. Trevor Cranston the respectable businessman who was always "only too happy to help the forces of law and order". In the manner of Jekyll and Hyde he would forget any reference to "Garth", his own corruption of Gareth, or anything symbolic of his true nature.

"Sorry I wasn't home when you called." he declared almost before the police and Customs officers had left their vehicle.

When the officers had introduced themselves properly they accepted Cranston's invitation to enter his office.

Cranston sat solemn faced as Colin Goodhew explained to him that a boat belonging to his company had been used in the conveyance of drugs which were banned from importation into the country. In the event that this connection meant some involvement in drug running by him or his company Cranston was warned by Goodhew to be careful in what he chose to say.

"It's got nothing to do with me. I can tell you that from the start but I'll help you all I can. I got no time for this drugs business, no time for it at all. Now, this boat, how do you know it belongs to the company?"

Cranston waved his hand in the air nonchalantly as he asked as if to accept that the officers were right in what they had said.

"The man we have in custody claims to have hired it from you." the detective constable revealed.

"Oh, now that is quite possible." Cranston replied, making a conscious effort to appear more relaxed. "We are quite happy to hire out boats that are not in constant use. That way we can get some sort of return on them. Have you any idea of the boat's name?"

He looked around him at shelves and desktops as if seeking something which was about to be useful.

"It is a launch about thirty foot long. It has the name 'Perseus' on the stern." the Customs man informed him.

"Right. I know that boat." said Cranston, rising to his feet and crossing to another desk. He opened a desk drawer and took out a small ledger which he brought back to the men. Crouching between the seated officers he leafed his way through the book, indicating to them occasional entries showing hire of the Perseus to R. Walsh for £30. The last of these entries fell on the previous day.

"See there he is right enough, just yesterday. I take it that's your man, this R. Walsh." Cranston said, enthusiastically prodding the page with his finger.

"Do you know him?" Goodhew asked evenly.

Cranston adopted a puzzled expression.

"Name don't mean nothing. If he comes about the boats I have probably seen him right enough, maybe even spoke to the guy but the name doesn't mean a thing, sorry."

Colin Goodhew gently took the book from Cranston's grasp.

"I'll require to take this book meantime Mr. Cranston. Just to show the hire of the boat to this man. It will be returned to you in due course."

"Happy to oblige." said Cranston resuming his seat.

"Perhaps you could oblige a little further." said Goodhew. "The receipt book which shows all these payments for hire of the boat, could I perhaps have it too?"

Cranston's smile disappeared momentarily and he looked decidedly uneasy. "I don't know if I can find that. It's eh....it's eh....it's someone else who issues the receipts."

Realising that his demeanour was doing nothing for his credibility Cranston rose again and crossed to the other desk. He made a vain effort to search the drawers for the receipt book but it was obvious that he would not find a book which had never existed.

"The money would only go into petty cash anyway." Cranston claimed. "I don't know for sure if the girls in this office ever bother with receipts for such things."

"Never mind it, Mr. Cranston." Goodhew said as he rose from his seat, scarcely able to conceal the inward amusement he had provided for himself.

Colin Goodhew had suspected that the ledger showing hire of the Perseus had been made up as a defence document in the event of Walsh being caught. Considering that Walsh could in fact have been caught on any of the drug trips it was reasonable to believe that entries in the book corresponded with drug running dates. The detective constable photocopied the entries from the book and kept them for future reference.

As the police vehicle drew out from the police office on its way to the court Ricky Walsh had only one unanswered question. How long would he spend in prison?

When the vehicle turned into the pend beside the court Walsh looked to the side and recognised the leather jacketed figure standing on the footpath. Quickly he raised his cuffed hands and with the thumb and forefinger of his right hand he made a gesture which he knew would be recognised by the ex-marine as indicating that all was operationally in order. It was what the figure in the leather jacket had hoped for. He turned and walked away.

Ten minutes later he was walking along the jetty with Cranston.

"Ricky hasn't told them a thing. Poor bugger'll be going away for a bit. His missus will find it a bit tight while he's inside."

"I'll see she gets provided for." Cranston said abruptly as if to suggest that he had previously considered the woman's welfare. "Just you don't go sniffing about her Norrie boy. Things is getting unstuck enough."

"Want me to take over from Ricky?"

"No. Charlie can do that but I have got a change in mind for you. You've been on that coaster long enough to get accepted. I want you on the lorries. I don't trust these bloody frog drivers."

Cranston's companion looked at him.

"They been short changing you?"

"No. I can't say that but I don't feel safe with them handling the notes and the gear. They could get ripped off at any time and it would take them a bloody week to tell us. I wouldn't know whether to believe them even then."

Both men laughed heartily. With the exception of legionnaires, they felt little respect for the French.

"It's not going to be easy trying to explain to this crazy bugger just what went wrong either." said Cranston, lifting an arm towards the large orange trawler that was approaching the jetty.

# FOUR

"Have a biscuit, Constable. I made them myself."

The old lady was obviously enjoying the company. Andy Fleming and Ian Pearson almost scattered her biscuits in their haste to comply with her invitation.

"Have you been in this flat for long?" Andy asked her.

"For the past twenty years," she replied, "and we have never had anything touched in this close in all that time. Only since that Masters family have moved in to the top flat have we had to put up with such noise, rubbish on the stair and now our coal is being stolen."

"It would be difficult to prove." observed Constable Pearson. "One person's coal is very much like any other person's coal. With such small amounts being taken from each coal cupboard can you be sure that it is being stolen at all?"

"I think the people above me are losing more than I am. They tell me but, like a lot of us old folk, they don't want a fuss so they don't tell you boys. For twenty years they have never needed to. We all feel a change for the worse, really. I was thinking of papering this room but now I wonder if it is worthwhile. Moving away seems like a better idea. My cat has been away for three days. She has never done that before." The old lady did not sound sad but she did sound fed up.

"Your biscuits were very good." Constable Pearson reported enthusiastically, having emptied the plate while the old lady was speaking.

"It is nice to have someone to share them with, apart from my daughter. She comes along on Tuesdays and Fridays. This must be Thursday. The Masters get these weird visitors every Thursday afternoon. They are all up there just now."

"We should go up and see." said Andy, winking at Pearson.

Pearson smiled and they both rose to leave.

The two officers climbed the common stair to the top flat where the door had a peep-hole fitted and the nameplate beneath it read "Masters". Beside the house door was the door of the coal cupboard and Constable Fleming noticed that it was fitted with a padlock.

Both officers listened close to the house door. They could hear laughter, conversation and the occasional chord on a guitar.

Andy Fleming gave the door an authoritative knock and the sounds from the interior stopped immediately. Someone approached the other side of the door and presumably looked through the security peep-hole. The officers heard some excited whispering. The toilet was flushed, someone called out to someone else, "In the fire. In the fire."

Only when this had all taken place was the door unlocked from the inside and then opened by Malcolm Masters. Behind him stood other men of similar age. From the hallway of the house came a sweet, musky odour.

"Yes." said Masters in the soft, mannerly voice which Andy Fleming remembered from their meeting in the alley. "Can I help you?"

Andy Fleming was deliberately polite and soft spoken as he explained.

"The old lady downstairs has become quite upset over her cat. It has been missing for three days. We wondered if you had seen anything of it."

Masters stared at the officer in cold disbelief.

"No. I haven't seen her cat." he replied in measured tones of great restraint.

"Well, now that you know about it perhaps you could keep an eye open for it. Don't bother looking in the coal cupboards though, she is keeping an eye on these herself. Good day."

The officers started down the stair and behind them the door was closed with what seemed like excessive firmness.

When he reached the old lady's door Andy Fleming gave it a gentle knock. The old lady opened it with a smile.

"If you can get in the wallpaper you want by next Thursday lunchtime, we will do that living room for you."

There was to be no negotiation. The old lady was given no time to object as the officers turned away. The old lady was shown the half-raised hand of farewell.

"Thank you." she whispered. "Thank you very much."

As they reached their vehicle Andy Fleming spoke quietly to Pearson.

"We have caught them cold today. Thanks to that little ploy they have probably just thrown about a hundred quid's worth of dope away but they will be more cautious in future. I want a note of all these vehicles parked here. You take the numbers on the far side of the street. I'll take these ones here but we'll do it from inside our own vehicle. No need to show them what we are doing. All right?"

"Aye sure." Pearson agreed. "I can do that all right. Wallpaper….that's another story."

When the men returned to the police office they processed the vehicle numbers and from the resulting lists they removed those of owners with neighbouring addresses to the Masters. All others had to be considered to be possible associates of the Masters and that would

THE WEED KILLER

almost certainly make them part of the local drugs fraternity.

The Chief Inspector had wanted his men to pay attention to the local licensed premises and while doing this Andy Fleming had noticed that a small side street pub, the "Drypuddle Bar", was frequented almost exclusively by a hippy clientele. He also noticed that, unlike other public bars, the place would have emptied by closing time and the customers seldom showed signs of drunkenness.

One night after closing time he had the opportunity to look through the place with the manager when the alarm bell was operated unnecessarily by a fault in the system. He had looked in the bins where the ashtrays were emptied and the cigarette ends drew his attention. He saw that they were from hand rolled cigarettes of the reefer type and there were enough of them to indicate that the smoking of cannabis resin on the premises had become commonplace. Such a practice could not occur without the full knowledge and complicity of the staff. By permitting it to take place they committed an offence. Andy stuck the reefer ends in his pocket.

He produced the cigarette ends and reiterated his thoughts to Chief Inspector MacKellar.

"If I can obtain a warrant to raid that place now, we can stop the spread of open drug abuse in the town. The courts would make an example of the licensee and other licensed premises would never want to run the risk." the constable reasoned earnestly.

"There will be no police storming of any pub, like something from an Al Capone film, not while I am Chief Inspector here. Do you realise that the licensee of the Drypuddle Bar is a friend of that retired law lord who wrote the article in the paper yesterday? He was condemning the Edinburgh licensing boards for their policy in respect of city centre pub licences. I have no desire to be the subject of his next article."

The Chief Inspector had nailed his true colours to the mast and Constable Fleming was disgusted by the attitude of a man who could rant and rage at his colleagues for one dirty footprint on the office carpet but was too political to take the proper action when it came to enforcing the law in his area. Making no effort to disguise his disgust Andy Fleming moved swiftly out of the Chief Inspector's office.

The following night he visited the Drypuddle Bar accompanied by Hamish MacLeod. He found the bar to be empty apart from the barman who looked bored as he rested his elbows on the draught taps.

"What's wrong tonight?" asked Andy, spreading his arms to indicate the unusual amount of space available.

"Maybe they heard that you were taking an interest in the place." the barman replied with a knowing smile.

## THE WEED KILLER

Hamish assumed that the barman was being sarcastic and gave a short genuine chuckle. Andy Fleming did not laugh but continued to look at the barman.

"And who suggested such a thing?" he asked without taking his eyes off the man.

"It was the boss who mentioned it to some of the staff and the word spread from there. I don't know where he got the idea." The part-time barman spoke plainly and sincerely.

"Thanks." said Fleming dryly. "Your boss has a silent interest in one of the hairdressing salons in town, has he not?"

The barman smiled. "Yes, and your boss has a wife who is less silent and likes to have her hair done."

Fleming and the barman looked at each other for a few moments before Fleming turned and left.

"Oh. You're here boys. Come on in."

It had taken the old lady a moment or two to recognise Andy Fleming and Ian Pearson out of uniform.

"I think I have everything you need."

She was certainly ready for them. Most of her furniture had been moved either out of the front room or left in the very centre. The previous paper had been removed by the old lady and her daughter on Tuesday and now the carpet was covered with old sheets. The kitchen table had been brought into the room and a bucket of paste was waiting beneath it.

On the table lay six rolls of wallpaper and a large pair of scissors.

It suited the policemen, turned decorators, to have the old lady in the kitchen as she herself suggested. As they worked both men kept a watchful eye on the street outside and whenever a vehicle pulled up Andy Fleming would rush to his 35 mm camera beneath the window. Concealed in a holdall bag the camera had a zoom lens and motor drive fitted in readiness to snap anyone heading for the afternoon meeting at Masters' flat. The visitors were wary and virtually posed for the camera by standing beside their vehicles while they searched the street for signs of the police.

Midway through the afternoon the old lady handed in a tray of tea and biscuits. The number of biscuits showed that she had not forgotten Pearson's appetite for them.

By five o'clock the job was over and the two men began tidying up the room.

"Thank you so much boys. You've done a wonderful job. You really have. I cannot thank you enough." The old lady kept pressing her hands together in delight as she surveyed the fresh pattern around the room.

Andy Fleming was certainly pleased with his afternoon's work. He had used a 36 exposure film and hoped to have a dozen faces to match to the identities of the vehicle owners.

Over the weeks he continued to take account of the persons who had roused his suspicions. He noted their acquaintances and the dates and times of their meetings. He discussed his observations with nobody. Pearson was aware of his interest and would pass on any observations of his own.

Felton Lang was one of those who had drawn his attention. Lang had moved to the area from Edinburgh only three months previously bringing his common law wife with him. She was an attractive girl trying her best to look unattractive. Her fair hair was in a pigtail which had not been undone for months and her clothes were loose, lengthy and extremely old. Andy had closed in on the couple as they shopped in the supermarket and had heard them talking. They were both soft spoken but she had an air of well-to-do and public school.

As far as Fleming could see, neither of these two were working and yet they ran around in a bright yellow van which was only two years old. They rented a country cottage and spent a lot of their time around the Drypuddle Bar.

Whenever he had seen the yellow van parked and unattended Fleming had taken a note of the mileage reading. From these it was apparent that travelling was normally confined to running in and out of town but an occasional lengthy journey was being made. Edinburgh perhaps.

A beautiful Sunday in the west highlands is worth two anywhere else and Andy got out the old Vauxhall to take the family around the back roads. It was there they could stop and enjoy the wonder of little known scenic beauty spots and discover fishing venues for some future evening.

As he drove past a small isolated cottage Andy braked suddenly. Mary and the children wondered what had gone wrong only to find that their driver's attention was firmly fixed on the vehicles parked beside the cottage. The bright yellow van was there but the vehicle beyond it had provided the surprise.

"Do you recognise that car at the back?" Andy asked Mary.

"Not really." she answered, realising that she had been expected to do better.

"That looks like the Cortina of our old friend the joiner. He must stay there." Andy informed her with some pride.

As the Vauxhall moved off again Mary wondered why the joiner's house should be so remarkable.

As Andy fell silent for a while he was beginning to realise how much of a grip this enquiry was taking. Sooner or later he was going to have to explain to Mary why they were spending more on petrol, more on telephone calls and his behaviour would occasionally seem to her to be a little bizarre.

He realised that he was no longer satisfied to simply wait and watch. He had set off early and come home late all in the interest of seeing for himself if particular cars were parked at particular addresses or certain individuals were taking public transport.

That night he satisfied his curiosity by looking in the voters roll. Fred and Janice Lord had stayed in that cottage for several years.

Two weeks later the bubble of secrecy burst between Fleming and his wife.

With the children at school, Mary had asked him to take her to Stirling. By early afternoon they had finished shopping and were on their way out of Stirling when Fleming braked and spun the car around. As they began driving back the way they had come Mary could not conceal her annoyance.

"What is it now?" she asked in a voice which suggested that no answer would be acceptable.

"I must know where that yellow van is going." replied Andy.

Of course she was entitled to know more and he told her. As he followed the yellow van at a safe distance he explained what he had been doing and what his suspicions were. Mary was in turn relieved, relaxed and then mildly interested.

The explanation had taken up some of the journey and by now it was apparent that the van was bound for Edinburgh.

Fortunately the address which provided the van's destination was in the west end of the city. Andy watched Felton Lang enter a house and took a note of the address. He then drove off without waiting for Lang's return.

"You better be back in time for these kids." Mary snapped.

He was.

A telephone call to the police in Edinburgh gave him the listed occupier of the address. It did not sound likely to be a relative.

Two days later came the telephone call from the Drug Squad in Edinburgh.

"Why were you interested in the house of Lukovic?"

Andy thought quickly. He resented being asked questions.

"I happened to be parked near to it the other day and I noticed several people coming and going. I thought I recognised one of them as coming from this area."

"Oh, I see." the Drug Squad officer sounded convinced. "That would be Lorn Allison from Aberdeen. He used to live in your area."

Fleming had never heard of Allison.

"Ah. You could be right. What would he be doing there?" Andy pressed.

"It's not a dealer's house as such," came the reply, "more of a dropping off point. Allison collects his stuff from it. So do guys from Glasgow and London. The meetings are irregular and brief. The stuff is never there for long. That's why we have never taken a chance on raiding it. We will some day when we can be sure of success."

"That all sounds very interesting." said Andy. "I hope you are lucky."

The blood tingled in his veins as he replaced the receiver. This was indeed interesting. He lifted the receiver again and dialled an Aberdeen number.

"Hello Kevin. Remember me, Andy Fleming? We were at the college together."

"Och, ah mind o' ye fine, Andy. Fit like? Y're a loang wyes fae whaur ye wis then."

"That's part of the reason for phoning you. I'm not long here and I want to know a bit more about a guy who stays in Aberdeen now but came from here originally. His name is Lorn Allison. I don't have an address, but perhaps...."

"Lorn Allison." Kevin shouted down the phone. "I can tell you aboot him. Naebody in Aberdeen can tell ye better than me aboot Lorn Allison. He is the biggest dealer in Aberdeenshire. He bocht his ain hoose during the summer. Paid it wi' cash. There's nae much ah dinna ken aboot him. He's a richt rogue."

Is it true that he came from here?" Andy asked quietly.

"Aye, that's true. I hiv a notee here someplace o' his previous addresses but he wis brocht up in your area. That much ah ken withoot lookin' it up."

"Kevin, could you be a real pal and send me down what you have on Allison? I think there may be a current drugs connection between him and here. I will let you know about that when I have looked into this a bit more."

The Aberdeen detective agreed and a few days later a package arrived from Grampian Police for the attention of Constable Fleming. Ian Pearson brought it to him.

"I thought I would let you open this yourself before someone opens it for you. You know what this place is like for 'opened in error' type nosiness."

"Thanks Ian, I appreciate it."

The package showed that Kevin had not exaggerated. He did know everything about Allison. Unfortunately the previous addresses were sufficiently previous that they now meant nothing at all. There was something of interest however, a list of telephone numbers which Allison had been calling on a regular basis. The STD code showed Fleming that three of the numbers were local to Corran Bay.

Excitedly, Andy grabbed for the telephone directory. He looked up Kasis B. and found it. No, it wasn't one of the three. He looked up Lang F. Yes, there it was. Allison had been calling Felton Lang.

The next number could be any one of the local circle. Andy decided to dial it. The number rang for ages before it was answered eventually, "Hello. This is Harry Manson."

Andy pencilled in the name as soon as he put down the receiver. Out of interest he called up directory enquiries and asked for Manson's number. He was told it was ex-directory.

The third number had a name beside it, "Tenny". Andy searched through the directory for any surname beginning with the letters TEN but came up with nothing. He dialled it and a woman answered.

"Sorry to bother you." said Andy. "I just wondered if Tenny was at home?"

"I'm sorry sir, I don't know anyone of that name. I think you must have a wrong number."

Andy did not wish to push his luck.

"Yes. I must have. I am so sorry."

Andy gathered up the Aberdeen papers and put them back into their envelope just as the detective sergeant came into the room.

"Hi Andy. The boss was hearing that you had made some enquiries about a place in Edinburgh and wondered what it was all about."

"How did he come to know that?" Andy asked with a frown.

"The guy you spoke to at the Edinburgh Drug Squad had assumed that you were a detective constable and phoned me to ask for the chap who was enquiring about Lukovic. He wanted to know how you came to be parked so close to that address. I didn't know anything about it so I asked the boss.

He was most annoyed because he knew nothing about it either."

"There's really nothing to know. I just happened to see something suspicious while I was parked." Andy explained dismissively, thinking quickly of what might have been said to the detective sergeant by the Edinburgh officer. "It seems that the business is between Edinburgh, Aberdeen, Glasgow and London. Nothing to do with here."

"And that parcel from Aberdeen? Is that just coincidence?" asked the detective sergeant in tones of disbelief.

"No. As a matter of fact I learned that an old friend of mine is working on something connected with the enquiry. His work is confined to Aberdeen but very interesting just the same. I may show it to you, after I've read it myself that is."

"So there is nothing to tell the boss." the CID man concluded.

"No. But while you are in the business of carrying messages you can tell him from me that my confidential conversations with him are having an adverse effect on the licensing trade. He may not know that but it would be better if our future discussions were confined to the weather forecast."

The detective sergeant turned with a broad smile on his face and made for the stair. The next five minutes would make his whole day.

## THE WEED KILLER

The Chief Inspector had realised that he would be better to allow Fleming some scope and agreed to search warrants for the homes of Masters, Lang and Kasis. The houses of Masters and Lang had been searched and small pieces of cannabis had been found in both.

Fleming crept through the rhododendron undergrowth of Fernshaw Estate until he found the gardener's cottage occupied by Benjamin Kasis. He studied the building from the outside, circling it at a distance. It was a long single storey building of white painted stone. The original thatched roof had been replaced by corrugated iron which had recently been replaced by thick tiles. Two large double glazed windows of a modern design had been inserted in the roof. Beside the end gable wall of the house sat the old van which Fleming had seen Kasis use to deliver a gas cooker to Manson. The road tax had expired and the vehicle would be unlikely to pass any mechanical inspection.

It was difficult to know what to make of Benjamin Kasis. He had a wife and a small baby. The gamekeeper on the estate complained of being poorly paid and it was probable that he earned more than Kasis. Kasis went infrequently to the Drypuddle Bar. He visited Masters' house regularly but Fleming had never seen him go near Harry Manson again since the handing over of the cooker. What was perhaps most interesting about Kasis was the way he was able to visit a building society office regularly. Fleming had asked Mary to follow him in one day. While she had enquired about child accounts she had overheard that he was depositing a hundred pounds.

This house of his would certainly be worth searching but so soon after searching Masters and Lang was not the time. Fleming would be patient.

Whenever a party was taking place at which drugs could be expected Fleming took out a warrant and raided it. Invariably he found drugs but it was almost as important to find diaries and letters. He kept details in the hope that time would bring the answers.

The summer nights were pleasant. When the revellers had left the local hostelries and the streets were empty of people, the seagulls moved in to raid the litter bins. Fish and chip wrappers, hot potato remains in polystyrene boxes and the odd discarded morsel were thrashed about in ownership disputes.

As the patrolling policeman approached, some of the scavengers flew off. Others grabbed an item of booty and ran at a fast trot to the opposite footpath.

Andy liked to make for the pier about three in the morning. It was then that the fishermen would begin to appear. Without noise or fuss they boarded their boats, started their engines, cast off and ghosted into the night with only their navigation lights to show their chosen course.

The boats held a fascination for Andy. He had a private desire to spend a few days at sea just to discover the fulfilment he had been told that it held.

He stared down at a small dark trawler called "Eilean Belle" and dreamed of having such a boat of his own. On a night like this he would drift off with the others. He imagined that Mary might have something to say about his idle dreaming and he smiled to himself. It wasn't her voice that brought him out of his dream but a deeper voice behind him.

"You can come if you want." the elderly fisherman said cheerfully. "Willie and me are just leaving."

Fleming turned to face the two men, both well into their fifties, who were heading for the edge of the pier.

"Is that your boat, the 'Eilean Belle'?" Andy asked them.

"Aye. It is." replied the same man. "It belonged to my father before me. Willie and me have been her crew for the past twenty years."

"I was just admiring her. These small trawlers are disappearing. Too old and too small to be viable nowadays, I suppose." remarked Fleming.

"She's over fifty years old right enough. Nearly as old as Willie and me but she'll see us off probably. She's a sister ship to that boat that disappeared a while back, the 'Beacon Belle'. They were both built together from the very same design, aye, and the very same wood, down Tarbert way." the older man reflected.

"So this boat is identical to the Beacon Belle." mused Fleming.

"Aye." said the old skipper, heading for the pier ladder, "Except this one's still on the surface. Poor Fergus. He never deserved to go that way. Bloody submarines."

Willie had hung back to cast off the mooring ropes.

"On you go down, Willie." said Fleming. "I'll do it. It's the closest I can get to going with you I'm sorry to say."

As the small boat moved away from the lights of the pier Andy Fleming looked after her with a spiritual sense of recognition.

The two days off following a week of nightshift are virtually useless as the time is spent recovering from the sleep debt of the previous week and the conditioning of mind and body to the idea of returning to normal living. Fleming refused to allow the disruption to affect his off-duty surveillance of those he had become interested in.

It was almost with relief that he was dutifully required to work dayshift hours for a couple of weeks. Mary had told him that if he wanted to speak to half the policemen in Britain about drugs then he should do it from a police telephone and try to get their own bills back to an acceptable level.

As he examined the custody records to learn who had been arrested during his days off Hamish brushed past.

"See your teacher got off light." Hamish commented.

"The cannabis oil man? Has he been dealt with?" Fleming asked incredulously. Cases were taking upwards of six months to go through the courts and death of young Stevie had been on Fleming's last nightshift just over a month previous.

"That's right." said Hamish. "He got fined fifty quid."

"WHAT?" roared Fleming in anger and disbelief.

"It's in the court returns. See for yourself. I haven't heard anyone mention it, they probably don't realise that it's the same man with the case being taken so quickly."

Hamish had taken out the court returns and looked up the entry he had seen.

"There he is, guilty to possession, fined £50."

Fleming stared at the entry, his eyes widening, his blood pressure rising.

"Give me that." he rasped impatiently and, grabbing the court sheet, he stormed out of the office.

The Procurator Fiscal threw himself back in his chair. It was now his turn to widen his eyes.

Constable Fleming had just materialised before him waving a sheet of paper in his hand.

"How can I explain what, constable?" gasped the bewildered and exasperated prosecutor.

"How did a schoolteacher who provided a young man with the means of getting himself killed manage to sneak through the penal system a month later with nothing more than a fifty pound fine?" asked Fleming, his face white with rage.

"Oh that." said the Fiscal, at last recognising and recalling the case. "That chap's solicitor telephoned me to request that his client be dealt with as soon as possible as he intended to plead guilty and get the thing over with. We discussed the nature of his plea and I was able to slip him in last week."

"Oh he slipped in all right, and he slipped out again. The one thing he didn't do was to slip up, we did that for him. Judging by the size of the fine it was never mentioned that he had supplied cannabis oil to a teenage boy who then got into such a condition that he threw himself in front of a taxi and died."

The rolled up court sheet was now being pointed at the Fiscal.

"I couldn't mention it because we couldn't prove it." the prosecutor replied with some emotion.

"You never tried to prove it." Fleming said coldly. "This man gave cannabis oil to a young man who had not expressed any desire to have any, never expressed any interest in it and when it was given to him he did not know what effect it would have on him. The teacher should have known but didn't feel up to telling him. He just buggered off and left the young man to die. Surely anything as criminal as that is worthy of proceedings? What have we done about this man? It has been a case of 'Tut-tut, old man, poor show. Give us fifty quid and we'll say no more about it.' Now this hero goes back to spouting Lord only knows what kind of education to the unsuspecting children of unsuspecting parents with no word of his irresponsibility or culpability. He does that with your blessing because possession is so easy to prove."

Fleming paused to regain his breath and some of his control. The Fiscal stood up.

"I appreciate the emotions of such cases as well as anyone. I feel them myself, although you apparently choose to disbelieve that. I am not empowered to put before the court a serious case where I know in advance that the sum total of my best evidence does not from the outset amount in law to sufficient proof to prove the charge. The youngster who was supplied the drug is dead. The cigarette, or any part of it, is not available for analysis or production in court. The dead boy's friend can identify the man who spoke to them. He can identify the container as like the one the man had with him but he never actually saw the man put anything in the cigarette. He is not a smoker and he rejected the cigarette from the start. There is no medical evidence to specifically show that a drug and not some other cause made the victim behave as irrationally as he did. So where's the evidence?"

The Procurator Fiscal paused to regain his composure and for a moment there was silence between the two men.

"I know how strongly you feel on the drugs issue." the Fiscal said quietly. "I can tell from the reports you submit and the attention you are obviously paying. I understand, and for that reason I will say no more about this little outburst of yours, but you must be careful to apply cold logic to this one-man crusade of yours."

Fleming stared back. Only now was he beginning to consider how far out of line he had been but he was not totally repentant.

"It is not supposed to be a one-man crusade you know. Senior politicians, lawmen and medical spokesmen all appear on television or in the press saying that greater efforts will be made to stamp out the drugs menace. Greater efforts? A young man dies and the net penalty is a fifty pound fine? How am I supposed to apply logic to this? But then again, you may be right about the one-man crusade."

Fleming had spoken in hushed tones, the fire of the past few minutes had been replaced by a tone of hopelessness. Now he turned and walked slowly from the Fiscal's office.

Behind him, the Fiscal sat down in his chair and leaned back, a little angry, a little drained, a little sympathetic but mostly understanding.

He was still sitting back when the police officer again stepped into the room.

"Sorry sir."

The Fiscal knew as well as anyone how long thankless hours could take their toll of a man.

"All right. All right, constable." he sighed with a wave of forgiveness and dismissal. "Next time count to ten."

After such a day there was only one way to spend the evening.

The lounge bar was fairly quiet but then Fleming had arrived earlier than most people were prepared to be. He sat in a corner and his mind raced from one topic to another but his thoughts seemed always to return to the death of young Stevie. How pointless, how senseless and how unpunished it had been. Was this the way society was headed? Wait till the drug pedlars have us by the throat? Fleming remembered his schooldays and those revered gentlemen who had done their best to educate him. Hard to imagine those men smoking cannabis reefers, hard indeed to imagine them with rucksacks on their backs.

"Another glass of malt, please."

What about all this supposed enthusiasm by the politicians too? Hypocrisy. It was politically proper to be opposed to drugs and stepping up to say so was all that they needed to do. What lay behind these fine speeches? Apathy. Every year figures were released to say how many murders there had been, how many break-ins, how many rapes and how many road accident deaths. These figures were enormous and realistic because they reflected both the detected and the undetected. How much smaller would they be if the undetected figures were deducted? Oh yes sir, there would be a case of congratulation, but drugs figures were already limited to detected cases. How could they be otherwise? What statistics would show the full extent of drug abuse in the country?

"Another malt please."

Nobody could ever turn to the police and say that they failed to find thirty five tons of cannabis or detect thirty million cases of drug possession. The only figures were for the detected cases and they were constantly said to be giving cause for concern. Figures which were probably only scratching the surface….and they were a matter of concern.

"Another please."

What about young Stevie? He would never be a drugs statistic, just a road accident statistic. Poor wee man.

"You should never drink on your own. Not the way you're drinking anyway."

Fleming turned towards the voice. She was an attractive girl, probably in her mid-twenties.

"Do I know you?" he asked, aware that his faculties were diminishing along with his money.

"No, you probably don't." she replied. "But I remember you. You were at the memorial service for the boys from the Beacon Belle."

"Yes. Yes, indeed I was. Sad business that."

"Why did you go to the service? Did you know the boys?"

"Yes. I read all ….. all that was written about them in the papers."

"You're a policeman. I've seen you about the town. Are you catching many criminals these days?"

Fleming leaned back in his chair and sighed.

"Not the ones I want to catch." he said with conviction.

"Another for me and….what will you have?"

"Just a martini please."

"You're not a married lady I hope."

"No. I have a steady boyfriend, a fisherman. He's at sea just now."

"I hope….I hope he's not one of these….not one of these buggers who are bringing….who are bringing in the dope."

"Shoosh." she whispered, looking about her. "You never know who might be listening. I have no time for the drugs either but there are plenty who do. Davy would never do anything like that. He hates them. I think he might know who is involved with them but he would never tell, not even me."

"I don't suppose he would….tell me?"

"No chance."

"Do you….do you want another one?"

"No thank you. And neither do you. I think you've had enough. Come on we'll get you home."

"That's very....very kind of you. What's your name young lady?"

"Loretta, Loretta MacAuley."

"That was some condition you came home in last night." Mary commented loudly from the kitchen.

Andy negotiated the bathroom door successfully and closed it behind him, hoping to make the room soundproof. As he tore the foil from a large fizzy tablet and threw it into a glass of water he tried to recall the previous evening. His mind went more readily to the argument with the Procurator Fiscal. The Chief Inspector might know all about that by now and provide a head-nipping lecture on the way to treat Procurators Fiscal. Andy considered that his head could scarcely be worse prepared for such a lecture. He fumbled his way through the morning ablution routine and wandered back to the bedroom to get dressed.

"Have you any money left?" Mary shouted through from the kitchen.

He visited each pocket of the previous evening's attire in turn and amassed the sum of....

"Two pounds, twenty seven pence."

"Is that all?" she shouted back in disgust. "I was hoping you would have enough left for a decent contribution to the retirement presentation."

"What presentation?" Andy groaned as he struggled with a black sock.

## THE WEED KILLER

"The old minister retires this Sunday. We have to pay our money to the elders by then. I had us down for £10." she said ruefully.

With his sock only half on Andy hobbled to the bedside cabinet and pushed his hand to the back of the drawer. He had kept a £5 note there since he had discovered it in the inside pocket of an old jacket. Now was the time to produce it.

He finished dressing and went into the kitchen.

"Here you are dear. It's actually more than I thought. Seven pounds and twenty seven pence."

"Oh well, at least that's more like it." said Mary thankfully. "How did you manage to have this much left when you obviously drank as much and then took a taxi home?"

I came home in a taxi?" he asked as he poured himself some cereal. "I don't remember paying for a taxi."

"Maybe you didn't." Mary said, laughing. "Do you remember anything of last night?"

Slowly the evening came back to him. The girl, what did she call herself? She looked lovely at the time. He wondered how she would look in the cool light of day. The conversation. He had begun to talk about drug running. He could remember that. What an idiot. How much had he said to this girl, this stranger with a boyfriend who was a fisherman?

His thoughts were interrupted by Mary as she sat down beside him and pushed a mug of tea in his direction.

"After this Sunday our own wee kirk will be closed until the new minister is chosen. We will be using the Parish Church in the meantime."

"You'll have to start rising earlier on a Sunday. The Parish Church is at the other side of town." Andy pointed out with a smile.

His wife always had difficulty reconciling her attendance at church with her desire to stay in bed on Sunday mornings.

"I will." his wife said with mock conviction. "You know they have commissioned an artist to paint our church. The minister is being presented with the painting on Sunday. The children are giving him a good dictionary and a book on birds. Apparently he does a bit of bird watching. Whatever is left will go to him in the form of a cheque so that he and his wife can buy whatever they wish. He isn't doing too badly at that, is he?"

Mary had expected her husband to be listening but when she received no response she realised that his mind was elsewhere. She watched him as he stirred his tea unnecessarily. It was almost as if he had hypnotised himself with the circular motion of the teaspoon. She wondered what he was thinking.

He wondered how much he might have told Loretta MacAuley.

# FIVE

It was now three weeks since Claas Van Dongen had heard from Robert Whelan.

The telephone rang.

"Hello Claas. Just to let you know that we are in business. From now on you will be dealing with MacArthur Whelan Finance, registered in Rochester."

"Very well, Robert, but I do not wish to discuss this particular business by telephone. You must come to see me and we can arrange investment."

The Dutchman had promised himself that complete caution would be exercised in dealing with Whelan.

"I will not manage down for about a week, Claas. I am very busy but all is going well. I hope to tell you more about it in a week or two. I will ring you in advance of my visit. My best regards to Mrs. Van Dongen."

"Thank you Robert. Till I hear from you then, good-bye."

Claas Van Dongen replaced the receiver and tried to convince himself that his feelings of unease were without substance. His thoughts were immediately disturbed as the telephone rang again.

"What? No I do not wish to receive the bills for the company to pay such things. If you wish to travel about the country by car I would find that difficult to reconcile with shell fishing. Send me an estimated account for creels, showing a reduction for cash payment. I will then reimburse you. I trust you can come up with a receipt from someone. When you come down here do not come to my house. If you telephone, we can arrange a rendezvous, somewhere private. How are things with you anyway?"

Van Dongen listened to a history of minor mishaps without any real interest.

"Nobody has their eye on you, have they?" he asked. "No. Well that's all that really matters. Be careful. Goodbye."

Once again he sank into reverie on the whole business. He stood in the centre of the room with the tip of his thumb between his teeth and that was how his wife saw him when she entered.

"Claas. What are you doing? You are going to be late for the Bridge Club."

Jacques Troutam cursed in English and French alternately as the swell threw his boat about on the Corryvreckan. An hour earlier he had made another successful delivery to Manson.

He had seen Manson speed off in the darkness. The swine would be home by now in that fancy speedboat of his.

Troutam spread the chart and barked instructions to his French mate. The mate took over the wheel and Troutam puffed on his thick cigar as he surveyed the chart and instruments to ensure a safe course into the lee of the Isle of Jura.

Constable Fleming walked towards the Lifeboat Jetty. He could see Pat Craig, the coxswain of the lifeboat, down on his knees adjusting the height of tyres suspended against the sea wall.

"The calm after the storm." remarked Pat, lifting his hand towards the clear blue sky.

"Aye. I heard it blew up a bit last night." Andy Fleming rejoined. "I also heard that you heroes were out in it all."

"We were out in it all right." Pat confirmed. He then stretched his arm towards the tyres he had been adjusting and continued. "I had the lifeboat alongside this wall to let the rest of the boys climb on board but she kept dipping below the tyres and scraping against the wall. I can't afford to let her do that too often. Any ideas?"

Fleming looked at the rough wall, constructed from roughly hewn granite blocks and shook his head.

"You need something that goes all the way down the wall in order to cushion a collision at all levels. You could hang a series of tyres but that wouldn't look very good. I'll think of something, Pat. I know the idea, I just can't think of a suitable item to achieve it."

The two men turned away from the edge.

"What was your call-out for?" asked Fleming.

"We had a pregnant woman to pick up from one of the islands. They never seem to want to deliver when the sea is calm." Pat said with his customary chuckle.

"Nothing else doing?" asked Andy, thinking of the unexpected nature of the short storm and the possibility of boats being caught unawares.

"There was a hell of a queer thing happened on the way back." said Pat, leading Andy into the Lifeboat office. He pointed to a spot on the wall map and continued. "We were just about here when the long scan radar picked up a vessel crossing towards Orsaig. We checked through the glasses but there were no lights. I tell you, Andy, that thing was shifting, heading straight for the south end of Orsaig. It was faster than the lifeboat, I'll tell you that. It disappeared off our screen ahead of us. We made no ground on it at all and we were flat out at the time."

"Did you look for it?" Andy asked with obvious interest.

"Yes. Once we dropped the woman off, we went back to the bottom end of Orsaig. It was possible that the thing had come to grief on the rocks so we crawled about there. Nothing showed on the radar screen so we killed

# THE WEED KILLER

our own lights and struck that power beam of ours over the rocks around the south shore. The wind had dropped by then but we still had to keep our distance."

"Did you see anything?" Andy prompted.

"No. We didn't see anything of the boat but the damnedest thing happened. As we shone into the rocks near Flashmore Cottage a lamp, like one of these hand held torches your traffic cops have, flashed back at us, three times. We thought we had found a shipwreck survivor." Pat chuckled again. "But when we shone our own lamp we never saw a soul. I called out over the loudspeaker that we were the lifeboat and gave a couple of turns of the blue lamp but there was no response."

"What did you do then?" Fleming wondered.

"What could we do? We spoke about it and we considered that we had done all we could do. I rang the farmer Archie MacGregor this morning and asked him to check out that corner for me but his own thoughts were the same as mine. The army and the SBS carry out operational manoeuvres around Orsaig at night. It might have been them, fast boat and all. We decided to leave them to it. They wouldn't welcome any intrusion or enquiry from us."

"No. You're right Pat. It was obviously somebody involved in covert activity who might have taken you to be one of them because your lights were out." agreed Andy, but not necessarily accepting Pat's explanation.

After a cup of tea with Pat, Andy left the lifeboat office and walked towards the pier. His thoughts were of Manson. Could it have been him? He stopped to speak to Donnie MacIntosh.

"Have you seen much of the speed merchant lately, Donnie?" he asked with a smile.

"Why, the man came by just an hour ago." replied Donnie. "Do you know I think he is still tied up at the pier. He does that you know. If he is going about the town on his own he leaves it and if he is away overnight he always leaves it at the fishing pier."

"I can't say that I've seen it left overnight." Andy said, frowning.

"Ah, but it has." insisted Donnie. "You just ask Norman."

Fleming had no intention of asking the pier master.

"Where could he go?" Andy asked aloud.

"He borrows a car sometimes. That old beat up Fiat, you'll have seen it." replied Donnie.

"Oh sure. He does his messages in that but what about going away. I don't think he would trust that old Fiat. I know I wouldn't. Anyway the guy who owns it uses it himself." Andy reasoned.

"Maybe he hires one." suggested Donnie.

"Yes." Andy said with a smile. "Maybe he does."

The only place in town which hired out cars was Watson's Garage.

"You say that he has just taken one out?" Andy asked of the little old lady who worked part-time as a booking clerkess.

"Yes, constable. He took a Ford Escort out for twenty four hours. Said he was going up north."

"You do keep a note of the mileage after each hire, don't you?" asked the police officer.

"Yes. We record it on the sheet. They have to pay for every mile over a hundred miles per day. It's in the agreement you see."

"Yes, I do see. When he comes back could you be pleasant to him and see if he will tell you where he has been? I would be very interested you understand."

"I do understand, constable. I'll speak to him."

The old lady looked the reliable sort.

"Oh. One other thing dear, did he take his wife with him?"

"No. Not this time, but he was asking about a car for next weekend for him and his wife to go south."

"Really? Well I will check with you next week as to whether he has confirmed the booking. Thanks for your help."

The elderly clerkess saluted the half raised hand as it followed its owner out of the door.

"And how much do you want for this worthy craft, young man?" Fleming asked.

The young fisherman looked down at the rubber dinghy he had repaired so often.

"It is still quite serviceable." he said, rubbing his chin. "I want a bigger one to do the creels. I would be happy with £60."

"Then £60 it is. Here is your money."

"I have done a lot of work on this John and I still cannot be sure if the people of today have any link with the people of the previous incident. You can help me."

It was a quiet Sunday afternoon and Andy had found John Grierson alone with time to talk. By now he hoped that he had convinced the big fellow that his interest was sincere and professional.

"What do you want to know?" big John asked, pulling out a cigarette and placing his size 12 boots on a nearby chair.

"Basically John, it would help to know of everyone you can remember from that previous incident. What you knew then about members of that team."

"Some of them were actually convicted and they should still be in prison." John began. "The ones who escaped are the ones I remember best anyway. The ringleader was the chap Whelan. He stayed on Orsaig with a man called 'Hippy Dan', I don't remember his real name. They went up north with a guy Brunton. I'm sure Brunton bought a fishing boat. Whelan went to Skye but then came back to the mainland and bought a hotel. Ballinbuck Hotel. It was a big old place. I don't know if he still has it. I've never seen him since but a couple from Orsaig reckoned they saw him on the pier here this summer. 'Hippy Dan' went south but I don't know where."

"So these guys just shot off when the game was up." Andy said thoughtfully. "Do you remember anyone else who disappeared at that time? What about the locals? What about Allison?"

"You mean Lorn Allison? Yes, he went to Aberdeen about then. I'm sure that chap Manson left here about that time too." John replied.

"Manson was here then? And he left?" Fleming asked with disbelief.

"Sure. He fished locally in a small boat. He was a bit of a loner but he knew these waters like the back of his hand. He left to go south but I could not really say that he was involved with the crew on Orsaig. The local men were very much on the periphery of things. Michael Bates the car salesman and Bert Ross the publican, they were said to be involved but it could never be proved."

"Why were they thought to have been involved?" asked Fleming.

"Before they went into business for themselves Bates was a clerk in an office and Ross worked aboard a fishing boat. Almost overnight they became business people. The Orsaig thing just seemed to provide the answer, at least in the minds of local people." John Grierson explained.

"Could they still be suspect?" Andy asked.

"I don't think so." John said seriously. "They are in good established businesses that pay well enough and they must realise the suspicion they would arouse by doing anything dodgy. No, I can't see either of them being that stupid."

"What do you think is going on at the moment, John?" Fleming asked openly.

"I suspect these fish lorries from the continent. They must be involved. Have you seen them take on shellfish at the pier? The crabs and lobsters are still alive. They go straight into big tanks of sea water to keep them alive for the journey south. The lorry driver pays the fishermen direct, in cash, usually hundreds of pounds. They weigh the fish of course but very few receipts are ever issued. The driver keeps a book of what money he is paying out but there is no strict control over the proceedings, no scrutiny at all."

"I have watched the fish being loaded." Andy said in annuent agreement. "I have mentioned it to the Customs boys and they say that they do the occasional spot checks on these lorries both here and at the south coast ports."

"They are not suggesting that they stick their hands down through tanks full of crabs. I can't see them doing that." John said with an expression of disgust. "I have seen the amount of checking they do here and I doubt if the drivers feel threatened. As for the south coast, the stuff will not reach there. What would be the purpose of bringing it in just to take it out again?"

"Are there any local guys on these fish lorries? All I ever see are these Spanish blokes and the odd Frenchman." Fleming asked.

"There is one stays not far from me. He is a bit of a hard case, Norrie Winston. He moved here from Haverford about a year ago. At first he worked on a coastal trawler but just a matter of weeks ago he started work on one of these big juggernauts that take the shellfish. He doesn't drive. He just sits with the driver and makes the payments. He tells me that he can be carrying up to £30,000 in cash at times. I get the impression that he is there to protect the driver and the money and anything else that might be on board."

"How did he get a job with a foreign lorry while he is staying up here?" Andy asked. He could not see the driver employing someone.

"He is employed by a firm in Wales." Grierson answered. "I don't know what the connection is. All I know is that he is staying in a bungalow that's been paid for. Unlike you and me, he has no mortgage."

"Have you ever seen him get visitors of any significance?" Andy asked.

"He hardly ever gets visitors but twice in the last twelve months someone in an old brown Rolls Royce has visited him. I never actually saw the person with the car, just the car itself sitting outside the house. I checked out the registration and it belonged to someone from down where Winston came from so I never bothered too much about it then. Maybe I should have been concerned but I do not remember the number or the name of the owner."

"Would you remember the name if it was mentioned?" Andy asked hopefully, having determined to establish the owner of this Rolls Royce.

"I think I might." the big fellow said quietly.

"Hello....C.I.D. please".... ...."Thank you".... ....

"Good afternoon Detective Constable Goodhew. Constable Fleming, Andrew Fleming, remember I phoned you about a month ago and you were telling me about the fast boat pick-ups from the Spanish fishing boat.".... ....

"Yes, he IS still here."...."I saw in the press the capture you told me to watch for. Well done. Congratulations."

Andy Fleming then listened with some pleasure to the account given by Colin Goodhew of a high speed chase through misty waters, the ditching in the sea of brown plastic water tight bales and the ultimate arrest by police and Customs of the skipper of a small fast motor boat.

"What about the owner of the boat? Did you get him?" Andy asked when the story seemed to have finished.

"Couldn't touch him, see. The boat is owned by a leisure company who say that it was leased to the skipper. They deny all knowledge of the boat's activities." Colin Goodhew explained.

"What about the man in custody, does he suggest that they do know?" Andy pressed.

"He chooses not to say. I can't say as I blame him. The leisure company is a spin-off of the Cranston Shipping Company and 'Garth' Cranston is not someone to cross. As well as his local shipping and leisure companies he has a shipping company in Jersey, a large yacht in southern Spain and an interest in some finance company."

"Does 'Garth' Cranston have a criminal record? What kind of guy is he?" Andy enquired.

"His real name is Trevor Gareth Cranston. He is a giant in terms of sheer physical size but he has no record to speak of. Any dealings I have had with him have been cordial enough. He is very plausible and polite to anyone in authority but I understand he is something of a 'godfather' in business. He could arrange accidents for anyone who threatened him. He surrounds himself with 'heavies', mostly ex-marines and they know their business. I doubt if they have the sort of criminal records they deserve. A bit of a Flash Harry too, our Mr. Cranston, with his gold rings, Rolex watches, crocodile skin shoes and the like. I suppose you know the type I mean?"

"Yes, I think I recognise the type." Andy Fleming said slowly. "Would he also be the type to run around in a brown Rolls Royce?"

"That's him." Colin Goodhew confirmed. "He has a private registration plate too. Have you seen him up your way?"

"No. But he may have been here. I will watch out for him and let you know.".... ...."Aye sure.... Congratulations again on that bust. Bye for now."

Monday passed without meeting John Grierson but on Tuesday forenoon the two men met in the yard at the rear of the police office.

"John. That brown Rolls Royce. If I told you the name Trevor Cranston, would it mean anything to you?"

"That's the name. Trevor Cranston. It made me think at the time of Cranstonhill in Glasgow. My old man once worked there. Yes, that's definitely the name."

"Now for the next question." Andy said, raising his forefinger to signify the importance of the answer. "You mentioned a possible sighting of the man Whelan on the pier during the summer. Could that have coincided with the visit of Mr. Cranston?"

John Grierson pushed his hat back on his head and stared at the ground for a few moments.

"I should be able to pinpoint the day I last saw that car. I'm sure the wife and I were going out to her staff dance at the time. Archie MacGregor the farmer was the one who told me about Whelan and he's not all that often on the pier. He might remember the day he saw Whelan. I'll phone him."

"Thanks John." said Andy, sounding cheery. Things just might be starting to fit into place.

The old clerkess at the garage had called to say that Manson had confirmed his hire of a car from Friday to Monday. He had also asked to have the mileage cost clarified as he would be travelling up to a thousand miles. On the return of his previous hire the old lady had been pleasantly inquisitive and learned that he had been to the Isle of Skye.

"My word, how nice to see you again. I was beginning to think you had forgotten all about me," said Agnes Fordyce with a smile.

The old lady had not received a visit from Andy Fleming for some time and had not expected him to call on a Friday.

As they entered the living room an attractive dark haired woman in her early thirties rose from a chair to meet the visitor.

"This is my daughter Moira." said the old lady with a hint of pride. "Moira, this is Constable Fleming. Remember I told you about him and Constable Pearson." Having said this she spread her arms towards the walls of the room.

"Yes. Of course I remember." Moira said pleasantly, taking Andy Fleming's hand. "That was very good of you and you did such a good job."

"It was a pleasure, but don't spread the word. I wouldn't want to have to do it too often."

They all laughed as they sat down. The old lady rose to go to the kitchen for some tea.

Andy Fleming looked at Moira and noticed her wedding ring. Hardly surprising that she should be married.

"Do you finish work early on a Friday?" he asked, trying to sound more polite than inquisitive.

"Yes. I finish at four o'clock on Friday afternoons. I can afford a few hours here with my mother. My husband doesn't finish till eight on Fridays. He manages a store."

"You visit on Tuesdays too, I believe." Andy continued.

"Yes. On Tuesday evenings my husband goes to his camera club so I come along to see Mum."

There had been nothing to suggest that Moira had family of her own so Fleming avoided the topic.

"What is your job?" he enquired.

"I am a secretary in the law firm of Paterson, MacEwan and Company. I work mostly with Mr. MacEwan." she said, adding quickly, "He deals with property cases."

She obviously did not want to seem to be part of the opposition where criminal cases were being defended.

She was not to know that Fleming was not so sensitive as to be influenced by such a circumstance.

"And do you find the work interesting?" asked Fleming, failing to see how such work could ever be interesting.

"Not really." Moira replied, pulling a face. "Mind you there are sometimes little breaks from the routine. I had to do my security guard this morning."

At this point the old lady returned with the tea and a plate of 'Mr. Pearson's' biscuits.

"Thank you very much." said Andy, accepting his cup of tea. "Sorry Moira. You were saying that you had been a security guard. What was that all about?"

"Well," began Moira, leaning forward in her chair. "You have probably seen that there are two or three empty shops in the Main Street for sale. We are selling one of them for £95,000. It is probably the biggest of the three."

Andy and Aggie nodded in agreement of the story so far.

"Just after we opened this morning a chap came in to buy it. He had one of those cheap brief cases that you can buy from the newsagents, the kind with the combination locks. He asked Mr. MacEwan if the shop was still on the market. When Mr. MacEwan said that it was he laid this briefcase down on the desk and opened it. He had the whole lot in cash, ninety five thousand pounds. I had to take it all to the bank."

"It must be unusual for that kind of money to be paid in cash." Andy Fleming remarked without being completely sure how unusual it might be.

"Unusual." said Moira in amazement. "I have worked for the firm since I left college and hundreds of thousands of pounds worth of business has passed through the office but I have never seen that kind of money in cash before. Mr. MacEwan didn't think he had either. I never thought Fred Lord would ever have that kind of money."

"Fred Lord." repeated Andy Fleming. "There can't be all that many Fred Lords about. Surely you don't mean Fred Lord the joiner? He stays in the little cottage on the back road."

"Yes. That's exactly who I mean." said Moira positively. "I know him well enough. We were at school together although he is a bit younger than me."

"How did he get on at school?" asked Fleming.

"Not as well as he should. He hung about with a group of hippy types. They grew their hair long and kept to themselves. Most of them are away from here now."

"Was Lorn Allison among them?" Andy Fleming offered in educated guesswork.

"Yes he was. Do you know him?" Moira smiled.

"No. I've only heard about him. I hardly know Fred Lord either but I wouldn't have thought he had ninety five pounds, far less ninety five thousand pounds."

"You're right." Moira laughed. "Old 'Tenny' must have found a rich auntie somewhere."

"What did you call him?" Andy asked with some excitement.

"Tenny." replied Moira. "It was short for Tennyson. Alfred Lord Tennyson. We called him Tenny since we first heard the name. You know the kind of thing you do at school? I don't suppose anyone calls him that nowadays."

"Oh you never know." Andy commented quietly, lifting his teacup.

Having identified Fred Lord as the 'Tenny' receiving calls from Allison, Fleming elected to spend more time observing Lord's home and his recently acquired shop.

It seemed that more and more of his time was being devoted to watching those who might be involved in drug trafficking than was being spent at home with his family. Mary was making the point more often these days that the father of young children should be spending time with them and not carrying out work for which he was not being paid. Indeed, Andy Fleming's work beyond the call of duty was taking away greater amounts of the money he was being paid. Telephone bills, petrol costs and photography were now supplemented by stationery costs as he kept records of his observations and information.

In the quiet loneliness of nightshift patrol these pressures played on his mind. There was no doubt that she was quite right. He should be spending more time at home with his children. His little girl no longer asked if he would come to see her dance with the highland dancing class, or to hear her sing with the school choir. His son did not ask him if he would be there when he played football, or there to go fishing with him or if he could fix his bike. Like most nights at bedtime, the children just assumed that their daddy would be working.

While he pondered these things in his mind Fleming almost failed to notice the short dark figure walking past on the opposite side of the street. He glanced across just as the man was directly opposite and, although the person had his head bent forward and his face hidden in the upward lapels of a jacket, Fleming seemed to recognise this man. The manner in which he was holding the front of his jacket and the quick, short steps of his walk were a memory from years back.

Fleming turned and followed the man at a discreet distance.

The figure maintained the same swift pace and never once looked round.

Eventually the man walked into a cul-de-sac and by the time Fleming made the street corner the man had disappeared from sight.

Fleming considered that the short space of time available to the man ahead of him was only sufficient for him to have entered the first block of flats on the left. Fleming entered the flats and climbed the stairs. It had been a dry night and there were no wet footprints to indicate where the man had gone. The names on the doors meant nothing to him and not every door had a nameplate.

Fleming knew that most of the flats were privately owned and rented out. Tenants came and went all the time and the accommodation was perfect for those wishing to keep a low profile.

As he walked back towards the centre of town he wondered about the person he had just been following. If only he had seen his face.

By the following night Fleming's curiosity had intensified. He made a point of being in the same place at the same time and was able to see the figure approaching from a distance.

Taking advantage of the distance between them, Fleming set off for the block of flats in the cul-de-sac. Satisfied that he was well ahead of the returning resident, Fleming began posting small folds of paper in the opening side of each door frame approximately six inches up from the ground.

He retired to the rear of the building and waited for the arrival of his 'friend'.

He did not have to wait for long before the front door of the common close closed behind the man. There followed the faint sound of footsteps on the internal stair but these quickly reduced to nothing. Fleming quietly entered the common close and began to climb the stairs, checking each door for a paper fold as he went.

Only when he reached the top floor did he discover a door where the paper fold had fallen from its position. He noted the address and left.

The following afternoon Fleming was able to learn that the owner of the flat was a Mr. Carmichael who resided near to Constable Grierson. On the telephone he informed Andy Fleming that the flat has been rented for the past two weeks but the name of the person renting it did nothing for Fleming's memory of the stooped figure he had seen going there at night. He decided not to discuss the 'ghost' tenant with Mr. Carmichael.

That night Fleming determined that he would satisfy his curiosity by direct encounter. He waited in a shop doorway and watched for the hunched figure.

At the same time as on previous nights the man came quick-stepping along the street. As Fleming stepped out in front of him he was obviously alarmed and a packet of bacon fell from beneath his jacket.

"Oh ho." said Fleming, bending to pick up the large packet of bacon. "Where did you get this?"

"From the hotel. I work there as a cook." the man replied, at last lifting his face towards the officer.

"Freshwater." Fleming exclaimed. "Frank 'Freshwater' Delby. How did you manage to get a job as a cook?"

## THE WEED KILLER

Andy Fleming now recalled the likeable rogue from the east coast who had a tendency to pop up anywhere there was water. He had worked on tugs, dredgers, paddle steamers and inshore fishing boats. He had a tendency to suffer from seasickness on longer hauls in deep water and this had earned him the nickname 'Freshwater'. Frank was now in his forties and behind him lay a string of convictions for minor and petty offences.

"Job Centre sent me along. I was on a coaster for a while, cooking like, but I got fed up with that. This wee job's all right. I get my supper out of it." he said, pointing to the pack of bacon.

"Aye, that will be right." replied Fleming. "You and I know Frank what the hotel manager would say if I took this back to him and asked him if you were supposed to have it. You've nicked this. What else have you got beneath that jacket of yours?"

Fleming had noticed that Frank had continued to hold up the front of his jacket.

"Aw. What the hell." moaned Frank, loosening his grip.

As the front of the jacket opened, Fleming could see packs of sausage, some morning rolls and a carton of eggs. He summoned the police vehicle.

"You haven't learned much since I saw you last, Frank." said Fleming. "This will cost you your job."

When Frank had been charged and locked up he asked to speak to Fleming.

As Andy Fleming sat down in the cell beside Frank Delby he could see that the man was nervous and worried. He readily acceded to his request for a cigarette.

"You've put me in deep shit here, Andy. No matter what happens I can hardly win."

"How do you mean?" Fleming asked quietly.

"This little job at the hotel is just filling in for me. I got another job lined up down south. I can't afford to be locked up in here. These guys will break my neck if they find that I got myself locked up."

"What guys are these? What has it got to do with them if you get locked up? You've been locked up before." Fleming argued.

"They don't know that." Frank protested. "They would never have given me this other job if they knew that."

"You'll just have to turn their job down." said Fleming plainly.

"Not now." Frank said with hopelessness in his voice. "They would just get suspicious and come after me."

"What kind of job is this you're talking about, Frank?" asked Andy Fleming, a little reproachfully.

"I can't tell you." Frank replied emphatically. "Not unless you promise to let me out of here right now."

"You know I am not the one to make such promises but I can see what I can do. It has to be worthwhile mind. What you have to tell me would have to be important."

"It is, Andy. It is, I promise you."

Fleming left him and went to make a telephone call.

"Right." said Fleming as he returned. "You must tell me what you know and then you can get out. This charge of theft will still stand I'm afraid but at least you could get out."

Frank looked a little worried.

"I couldn't afford to appear in court and if I didn't appear in court there would be a warrant. If somebody came looking for me down there with a warrant, I'd be dead."

"Listen Frank." said Fleming, a little exasperated. "All this talk about how somebody is going to kill you isn't going to impress me one little bit until you can explain to me why anyone would want to kill you for stealing enough breakfast for four folk."

"These guys are not dealing in bacon and eggs." whispered Frank resignedly. "They are dealing in dope."

"And this job they have offered you is part of their set-up?" asked Fleming.

"Yeah. It pays well but now that I know about it I have to be cleaner than clean. They told me that, Andy. Cleaner than clean or deader than dead."

"What did they tell you about this job of yours?" Fleming enquired.

"Just that I was to operate a ferry service from one boat to another. Not here. Somewhere between Wales and the Channel Isles."

"Is that all they told you?"

"That's all. In fact they never ever said it was drugs, I just know. They're talking about £500 for six hours work every other week, plus any honest work I can find."

"When do you go?" Fleming asked.

"In a week or two." Frank said quietly. "Apparently they lost the boat they were using. They're hoping to buy another one to replace it."

"They lost it?" said Andy with a chuckle. "Is that what happened?"

"All right then, Frank. You can go but I want you to keep in touch with me, especially if you have to leave, so that I can do what I can to prevent a warrant chasing after you."

"I'll do that. I won't leave without getting in touch."

"I've never seen that wee kirk as busy."

Mary had met with the retired minister and they were discussing the presentation to him when Andy Fleming joined them.

"Hello sir. Have you moved to your new home yet?"

"No." replied the minister. "It is a nice little cottage but it needs quite a lot of work before it will be ready to live in. I do not need to hurry just now. I don't think the old manse is being used any more after I leave."

The old man dipped his head and took in a deep breath.

"My whole world is changing. A different house after all these years. I will have no right to be visiting the elderly and infirm without seeming to step on someone else's toes. The schoolmaster says he would like me to continue to visit the school but he will soon retire and after that I dare say I won't be welcome anymore."

"You will be more than welcome to visit us any time you are passing." Mary assured him. "But I cannot imagine that you will be short of things to do. I am hoping that we shall hear you delivering sermons whenever some other minister is absent for any reason. You are not exactly a stranger in this area."

"No. I suppose you're right Mary. I just feel a lack of purpose now."

"You must never think of yourself as having no purpose." Andy commented. "Not as long as your wife needs you to push one of these trolleys round the supermarket."

"You're right." the old minister agreed. "Even that seems to be taking longer nowadays. Talking of shopping, I better move along. So nice to have seen you both."

# SIX

Andy pulled open the doors of the derelict garage. He tried not to break the surrounding silence even if he did not really believe that there could be another living soul within a mile of him. The old Vauxhall was then rolled forward to fill the dilapidated building. Andy closed the doors behind it, feeling reasonably confident that nobody would suddenly become inquisitive about an old garage on a single track coastal farm road.

The night was dark and clear but he hoped to become acclimatised to the darkness and to see as well in the dark as the natives of Orsaig.

He pushed the small inflatable out from the shore until it floated freely in the shallow water's edge. Climbing into the dinghy he pushed against the shingle with the wooden oars and glided out in the level stillness. He had chosen a time of slack water and, with no wind to speak of, he hoped to navigate his way to Orsaig without problem or detection.

# THE WEED KILLER

If Chief Inspector MacKellar had been there to see Constable Fleming at that moment, he might have had a few questions to ask, that is, if he had somehow managed to recognise him. Fleming was dressed entirely in black clothing which included a balaclava and he had applied a dark facial camouflage paste borrowed from a friend in the Territorial Army. His own mother would not have known him.

It took only minutes to reach Orsaig and another five minutes to reach a gorse bush near the water's edge. He tied the dinghy to the bush and set off inland. He held a small, powerful torch but hoped to manage without it as he crossed towards the silhouette of the highest point on the island. By doing this he knew that he would meet with the dirt road which led south from the ferry point. He had studied the map of the island for physical features and for reference he had prepared a small photocopy which he now carried in his pocket stuck to a piece of cardboard.

His heart pounded in his chest and he imagined he could hear it as clearly as a drumbeat. For seventeen years now he had done his job in a totally orthodox manner and had often achieved the results he had been after. He now pursued an enquiry which defied orthodoxy and in order to see what he could already smell he was being forced to use covert methods.

He was personally convinced that Manson and his associates were engaged in drugs trafficking and had been responsible for much worse but their deeds had been veiled in legitimate behaviour. While this criminal activity remained subliminal Fleming would not receive the full backing of his senior officers to take orthodox steps against it.

The motto of the Flemings is 'Let the deed show' and Andy Fleming intended to do exactly that, even if he ran the risk of losing everything he had previously worked for. What satisfaction could there be in only counting as success the detection of matters which were all too obvious?

With surprising ease he found his way to the cottage. Before approaching it he looked around at the next nearest cottages until he was entirely sure that he had found Flashmore.

He crept to the house without disturbing the hens and ducks. The front door was locked as he had expected but one of the windows had been left open for ventilation. It had been that way for many years and a great deal of effort was required to open it far enough for Andy to climb through.

The interior of the house was in a filthy condition for it was apparent that the farmyard animals were being permitted access to the cottage.

After a cursory search of the house, Andy concentrated on the old hardwood bureau beneath the telephone. It was a mass of letters and papers. Fleming lifted each one of these in turn and glanced over them by the light of his torch before laying them on a nearby chair.

The letters were mostly family correspondence and demands from the factor for unpaid rent but they had to be removed before the address book became visible. Leafing through it, Andy could see that the entries were too numerous to copy but some were obviously significant.

Taking a small notepad and pencil from his pocket he copied some of them down. Jacques, Claas, Norrie and Ewan all had exchange codes he did not recognise. He suspected that Kiefel with an Edinburgh code might be Lukovic. The local numbers were also interesting. Felton Lang, Benjamin Kasis, Fred Lord, Malcolm Masters and Norrie Winston all appeared and Fleming was interested to see that Norrie Winston had been known by Manson before he came to stay in the area. He was also surprised to see that Manson had the numbers of Fred Lord and Malcolm Masters for, like Norrie Winston, they were people who had never been seen in company or conversation with Harry Manson.

Andy Fleming put the address book back onto the bureau and covered it with the papers from the chair. He pushed his notepad and pencil back into his pocket and picked up his torch. He was a little frustrated not to have discovered more.

He looked about the cottage with sparing use of his torch. The year planner calendar, pinned to the back of the kitchen door, was almost neglected for it appeared at first glance to have no entries made on it. On closer examination Andy found that a cross had been made in pencil on dates throughout the year. These dates were consecutively four weeks and six weeks apart. On dates following within a week of the marked dates an entry had been made to show a price paid for shellfish. Taking out his notepad again he copied the dates and figures from the calendar.

Looking at the current weekend dates, he saw that these had been marked 'Claas'. Manson had gone to see the man who owned the 'Hand Maiden'.

Andy left the cottage as untidy as he had found it and slipped away into the night without disturbing anyone. The islanders had told stories of dark shadowy figures in the night and had always attributed their observations to operational training by the armed forces. Any chance encounter would be explained in a manner consistent with their expectations.

Boarding the inflatable he felt more confident. His eyes had become used to the dark and he could see the 'Hand Maiden' a hundred metres to the south where she turned on her mooring. Andy rowed towards the boat and boarded her.

The cabin was locked but Andy shone his torch through the window. The interior was very well equipped and more tidily kept than the cottage. Everything seemed to be as it should and Andy had almost switched off his torch when a thick piece of shiny wood caught his eye. It protruded from a shelf space beneath the control switches. Moving around the outside to another window Andy shone his torch into the shelf space and was able to see more of the item. It was a double barrelled shotgun.

As far as Andy Fleming knew, Manson did not have a shotgun certificate. Why would he want a shotgun on the boat? Bearing in mind what he knew and suspected of Manson's association Andy considered that in Manson's position he might find a shotgun to be something of a comfort. Assuming that it was not for use against the law, its presence said much about the people Manson was involved with. Slipping back into his dinghy Fleming struck out against a falling tide.

At five o'clock on the following Monday morning Andy sat in the old Vauxhall watching the coast road. A mile down that road was the ferry crossing and the first ferry would be at six.

It was a beautiful morning and already bright enough for the taking of photographs. Sitting alone in the stillness he was feeling the effects of lost sleep but his head jerked upwards as he heard the sound of an approaching car.

The dark blue Ford Sierra was not travelling fast and Andy could readily make out the unwashed features of the driver. Travel weariness was doing nothing to improve the looks of Harry Manson. The pale diminutive figure of his wife was sitting beside him.

When the car had passed him Andy left his own car and walked to the bend in the road. By looking obliquely down the coast he could see the jetty where the ferry from Orsaig would shortly call. He saw the Sierra stop there and deposit Manson's wife and a couple of suitcases before turning back towards town.

Andy felt disappointed. He was not sure what he had hoped for, but from Manson he had expected something more than a normal homecoming. A stranger perhaps or some equipment, anything that could be photographed, that was what he had hoped for but now he wondered why he had bothered to rise at four in the morning with camera prepared just to witness a quite unremarkable return.

As he drove off towards home he scarcely looked at the figure operating the cash dispenser of the Clydesdale Bank or the parked Sierra. Manson would leave the car keys and the payment through the letter box of the garage before returning on foot or by taxi to the ferry point.

With so few people around any further surveillance could be risky. There were a few cars on the road at this early hour but it was unusual to see a taxi making its way into town.

Fleming was again beginning to tire and his failure to recognise the pale green Granada taxi he put down to the constant turnover in vehicles used by local taxi firms. The roof sign was a different design from those favoured locally. It ran the full width of the car roof and could easily take the words 'Bon Accord Taxi Hire'.

The old Vauxhall shuddered to a halt. It was then frantically manoeuvred around in the roadway in order to follow the taxi.

'Bon Accord' surely had to be an Aberdeen firm and to Andy Fleming Aberdeen had come to mean Lorn Allison.

He drove to Watsons Garage and saw the Ford Sierra parked in the forecourt. The garage was deserted.

He drove to the coast road and stopped at the first bend. Looking down towards the ferry point he could see Manson's wife pacing to and fro' beside her suitcases. The small ferry boat was pulling out from the jetty on Orsaig and would take only minutes to arrive. Manson was not there to meet it.

Fleming listened. Somewhere on the pier a diesel engine was running.

Fleming drove to the entrance to the pier and parked behind a large container. Grabbing his camera he ran behind the sheds and piles of nets to reach the rear of the marketing shed. Beyond the building he could see the Aberdeen taxi with only the driver inside. Turning the corner and crouching behind a stack of fish boxes Fleming could see Manson and another man in conversation. This second man certainly appeared to be a lot more refined than Manson. In his early thirties and dressed in expensive looking clothes he was speaking expressively but too quietly for Fleming to hear. Focussing his zoom lens on the pair Fleming switched on the motor drive and took a series of poses which would make recognition of Allison a simple matter for those who knew him.

Fleming concluded the film with two shots of the taxi and its driver.

As he retreated towards his car Fleming heard the taxi start up. With Manson and Allison aboard it sped off the pier and down the coast road. It returned a few moments later and drove out of town with Allison still in the vehicle. Fleming followed it until he felt satisfied that Allison was leaving his area. A telephone call to Kevin in Aberdeen would later confirm that Allison had gone home.

The house was silent. The kids were asleep and Mary had gone to bed. The television had been switched off. Andy Fleming sipped his whisky and dry ginger as he contemplated the facts resulting from his surveillance and enquiry.

A fisherman with poor returns from fishing was using an expensive and powerful boat while residing in a filthy cottage which had coincidentally featured in a previous drugs importation case on the same island. He had some sort of relationship with a foreign businessman in the south of England and a known drugs dealer was prepared to travel from Aberdeen to meet him as soon as he returned from a visit to his foreign friend. A drug dealer who had mutual connection with a dropping-off address in Edinburgh through an unemployed hippy who was friendly with a joiner who could buy a shop for cash.

Surely this was all too significant to keep to himself? Fleming wanted to be convinced that he was not viewing his facts with paranoia. If, as he now felt, it was time to reveal his observations to those chiefly engaged in the drugs ring-busting he did not want it pointed out to him that other innocent explanations were available.

In presenting his account he could not reveal the evidence he had found in Manson's house and boat. As a cop he would be expected to deal with Manson for having a shotgun without certificate and he certainly would not be excused his illegal entry to Flashmore. While these were matters which had enhanced Fleming's own suspicion they would have to be kept to himself.

In a cardboard folder he had stored paper cuttings, tide tables, scribbled notes of dates, places, registration numbers, telephone numbers and almost every type of fact which might prove relevant to his interest. Draining his glass, he began to pick his way through these papers until, beneath the others, he found a press cutting from the 'In Memoriam' column of the local paper. It was an entry placed by the family of a young fisherman, Roddy McCuish, to mark the first anniversary of the disappearance of the 'Beacon Belle'.

Fleming rose and went to a drawer of the rosewood unit. He took out the old diary which had lain there with no attention paid to it since before his removal to the new house. He took down a current calendar and returned to his chair.

He compared the notebook list of dates copied from Manson's year planner with his own calendar. From the calendar he continued the pattern retrospectively into the preceding year using the pages of the old diary until he came to the last of his own diary notations. He read these last entries and then looked at the date mentioned in the press cutting. He laid his head back against his chair and in his mind's eye he could see a previous year planner with the date of the Beacon Belle's disappearance marked with a pencilled cross.

"More coincidence." he muttered to himself.

He returned the calendar to the wall and opened the unit drawer to return the old diary. In the drawer he saw a small pile of letters held in an elastic band. He lifted them out and poured himself another whisky and dry ginger.

"You cannot tell me anymore, old friend, but let me look again at what you have already said."

Four hundred miles further south Trevor Cranston was enjoying a whisky in the company of Norrie Winston.

Winston had assured him that there was nothing to worry about at the Scottish end.

"If someone started rustling their sheep they would notice but our operation seems too sophisticated for them." Winston reported with more than a hint of sarcasm.

"I wish that was the case here." Cranston replied. His accent was the only indecisive feature about the man. His upbringing had been shared by separated parents, one Welsh and the other Liverpudlian. His voice carried a mixture of accents which altered in balance to favour the person listening.

"No news so far about Walsh." he continued. "Heard nothing from him. The poor bastard will be away for years. He isn't the type to talk, thank God, or I'd be away with him."

"You lost the gear too." observed Winston.

"Yeah. Nearly forty grand's worth. I'm not too happy about that but at least we're still in business. I'll get a loan from one of Whelan's finance companies and pay it back over the next two runs. You can expect something from Troutam and Manson next week.... if the Customs don't know about it."

"That's a point." said Winston. "How do you suppose they knew about Walsh?"

"Damned if I know." replied Cranston. "The only people I told were Troutam and yourself. On the pier, remember? The day the engineer was working on the boat."

"We were all stood in front of the toilets." Winston remembered. "You never said all that much really.

I remember you said that the cost of the gearbox could be paid if Walsh made the pick-up that night. That was all you said to me anyway. I never said a thing to anyone and I'm quite sure that Jacques wouldn't say either."

Winston had recreated the moment perfectly and Cranston was able to re-live it in his mind. Rubbing his glass against his chin he reflected on the memory.

"Norrie, did you go into the toilet at all?" he asked.

"Yeah sure. I went in just as we split up."

"Was there anybody in there?" asked Cranston, still rubbing his chin with the whisky glass.

"No. It was empty." said Winston immediately but then his memory improved. "Shit. There was somebody. An old guy came out of the cubicle when I was using the john. A guy in a blue knitted hat but I never got a good look at him."

"Sponge." breathed Cranston, his eyes widening.

"Did you see him?" Winston asked cautiously as he saw Cranston's fingers begin to squeeze the whisky glass.

"As a matter of fact I did." Cranston replied. When you went back to the lorry Jacques and I went for a pint of beer. That old bastard was in the phone box at the end of the pier."

Cranston put his glass down so firmly that he spilled some of its contents. He sucked the whisky splash from the back of his hand and reached for the telephone. He dialled a number that was well known to him and drummed his fingers as he waited impatiently for an answer.

"Hello Gerry, 'Garth' here. Listen Gerry, you know that old guy Sponge? He comes into your place from time to time when he has a few bob. Has he been in much lately?"

Cranston listened with great interest to the reply.

"Thanks Gerry, you're a pal old son. That's one I owe ya."

As he slammed the phone down Cranston showed the satisfaction of a man who had been proved right.

"That old bastard's been in the boozer every day since. He has more money now than Gerry's ever seen him with and a couple of times he has toasted the health of Ricky Walsh. Doesn't that tell you something Norrie lad? That old soak has sold his last bit of information."

It was mid-afternoon and a dampness hung over the city of Edinburgh.

Sidney Bowman Crosswell left the Lukovic flat feeling happier than when he arrived. He always felt safer carrying money, even £15,000, than he did carrying slabs of Pakistan Black and packets of heroine. Now all he had to do was make it back to the London train. He didn't like Edinburgh. It always rained in Edinburgh.

A dark saloon with a taxi roof sign came slowly down the street towards him. He hailed it and climbed in when it stopped.

"Waverley Station." he advised the man in the cloth cap.

"Nae problem, sir." came the reply.

The radio fed the room with noise. The two men faced each other over a coffee table.

"Lucky if this will last ten days." remarked the man with a hint of north-east accent as he stuffed small packets of heroine into his jacket pocket. He reached towards the cellophaned slabs of cannabis but was interrupted by the entry of two heavily set men.

"Scottish Crime Squad, gentlemen. We have a search warrant Mr. Lukovic."

"I no heard you knock." grumbled Lukovic.

"Perhaps if you were to turn down your radio you would hear someone knocking on your door. I'm afraid Mr. Crosswell forgot to lock it behind him when he left."

Kiefel Lukovic groaned.

Gerry Cutler pushed another whisky towards the old man. He had known him for several years and had seen him become a slave to drink. Gerry even knew that the old man's real name was Alan Catterson but most people simply knew him as 'Sponge'.

"You must have spent the best part of a hundred quid in here lately, Sponge. Win it at the dogs?"

"Sure, oh sure." the old man groaned. Sponge was drunk and did not want to discuss where his money had come from. He rose and staggered to the door.

Cutler watched him go and shook his head sadly.

"Now it's the dogs. The other night it was the bingo."

Once into the street Sponge made his way down the footpath cursing the distance between him and his coal cellar home. Something was troubling his fuddled brain. All week Gerry had been asking him questions. Where had he won the money? Had he heard about Walsh? It was as if Gerry suspected something and was trying to confirm it. Was Gerry really that interested or was he trying to get answers for someone else? Something was wrong, he could just feel it.

If he had noticed the Daihatsu pickup following him he would have realised how right he was. Douglas Road West was virtually uninhabited as it played host to storage warehouses but had no business or residential premises. It was dimly lit and Sponge chose to walk down the centre of the road. That was when the Daihatsu accelerated.

The time was passing slowly for Fleming. The hour and a half he had spent behind the hedge had seemed like a whole evening. Fred Lord was at home, or at least his car was, but nothing had happened since Andy's arrival at seven o'clock.

It was colder now and threatening to rain. He looked at the cottage once more and seriously felt that the time had come to call it off when he saw the cottage door open. Fred Lord came out of the house wearing a 'donkey' jacket and did not make for his car. Instead he walked down the road for a hundred yards until he came to a public telephone kiosk.

As Fleming watched, Lord went into the kiosk and stood inside. Why should he use a public telephone when he had a telephone at home? Perhaps his own was out of order. In the distance Fleming heard the phone ring briefly.

It was eight thirty-five on a Wednesday evening.

Fred Lord spent almost ten minutes on the telephone before returning to his house. Fleming waited another half hour in case Lord had been inviting someone to call at his home. No-one came but the time had not been wasted. Fleming had been considering why Lord should be receiving calls on an outside telephone when Kevin's information had shown that Allison was calling him on the house telephone. Was he keeping something from his wife? A girlfriend or a gambling arrangement, something of that sort? Fleming went home.

He checked the number in Kevin's correspondence against the telephone directory yet again and found Lord's number was the same in both. He dialled it himself and Mrs. Lord answered.

"Hello. It's Jim here. Is Cathie back yet?" said Fleming trying to sound young and cheerful.

"I'm sorry. You have the wrong number." Janice Lord replied.

"Sorry." apologised Fleming, replacing the receiver. "And you have a telephone that is working."

It was raining heavily now.

Where the raindrops struck the road surface they were thrown upwards in a spray. Where they landed on Alan Catterson's heavy coat they were absorbed immediately. His nickname of 'Sponge' was as appropriate in death as it had been in life. His wretched cadaver formed a dark wet lump on a dark wet road.

When the light of dawn invaded the street the old man would be discovered but the red rivulets heading powerfully for the gutter would be running clear long before then.

The manager of the marina was dwarfed by Cranston and Winston as the three men stood in the drizzling rain. Together they peered over the edge of the quay at a 26' fishing boat.

"Well worth six grand." the manager declared. "The engine's sound and there's a 25 horse outboard goes with her as well."

"You'll get five grand. That's in cash and only when you've had the bugger out and painted her a different colour." Cranston growled.

"Oh very well." the manager agreed meekly. "What colour would you like?"

"I don't give a damn what colour it is," roared Cranston impatiently, "just as long as it's different. Remember if anyone asks, it isn't me that's buying it. I'm just paying for it. The new owner is a guy from Scotland, a Mister....what's the bugger's name, Norrie?"

"Frank Delby." Winston replied.

"I understand." the manager said submissively. "The boat will be ready for Mr. Delby in a week." He paused to look up at the rain clouds. "Or maybe two."

"Better get this guy of yours down here soon. Charlie's too good to lose. Think this Delby character could handle that boat single-handed?" Cranston asked Winston as the two men made their way back to the car.

"Shouldn't be a problem for him at all." Winston confirmed.

As the two men climbed into the brown Rolls Royce neither of them paid any attention to the small red Ford Fiesta parked on the opposite side of the street.

Colin Goodhew was interested in Cranston's visit to the marina and had watched the conversation among the three men. He had not spent all his time watching them, for he had wanted to check the front of the Rolls for recent accident damage, but he had seen enough to be satisfied that the conversation had centred on the old fishing boat below the quay. As the Rolls pulled silently away, Goodhew alighted from the Ford and crossed to the boatyard at the entrance to the marina.

As he knelt on the edge of the quay he was approached by the marina manager.

"Mr. Delby?"

"No." replied Goodhew, a little taken aback. "No, I am not Mr. Delby. Is this boat for sale?"

He pointed to the fishing boat.

"No." replied the manager emphatically. "Mr. Delby is the owner of the boat. It is not for sale."

"You obviously do not know Mr. Delby when you could mistake me for him." Goodhew observed. "How do you know he is not selling it?"

"Because he has only recently bought it." the manager said with measured annoyance.

"Where could I see this Mr. Delby?" Colin Goodhew persisted.

"You can't. He stays in Scotland. He won't be here for a few weeks yet."

"Too bad." replied Goodhew, walking away.

"Hold on young lady, I want a word with you."

The voice was clear and authoritative and not at all the way she had heard it last, but Loretta was not too surprised when she turned to find Andy Fleming striding towards her. His voice dropped to a whisper as he reached her.

"Am I not due you the cost of a taxi fare?" he asked.

"No. You paid it before we left." she answered.

"Before *we* left." he repeated, a look of bewilderment on his face.

"Yes. I went with you until the taxi dropped you off and then it took me home." she explained in her 'don't you remember?' voice.

"I started to talk about drugs. Just how much did I say?"

She gave a short laugh.

"Plenty. But don't worry about it. I doubt if anyone else could have made out what you were saying."

Fleming groaned and shook his head.

"I know you would like to nail the guys who are bringing in the drugs. I am not sure that many people here know any more about it than you seem to know but I'll pester Davy into telling me anything he knows or gets to know from the other fishermen. It won't be much. The fishermen are not really involved themselves and Davy is never one to talk too much about that kind of thing. Still I'll let you know anything I do hear."

"Thanks Loretta. You sure I paid the taxi, I don't remember it?"

"I'm sure. I can remember, but then I was sober."

"Aye, all right." he said. "Point taken."

"See you." she sang as she skipped away from him.

"Sure." he said softly, half raising his hand towards her.

"And is your information recent?"

The old Justice of the Peace pored over the warrant with every indication of judicial concern.

As his eighty-year-old eyes peered through his pince-nez spectacles to where his eighty-year-old forefinger followed the printed text with occasional derailment. His breathing was the only sound to be heard.

He was mannerly and respectable and Fleming liked him a lot. It was obvious that being asked to grant a search warrant made the old gentleman feel important, useful and wanted. Such things mattered a lot to a man who had once been important and useful in his younger days and had always been wanted, certainly by the lady he had survived by ten years.

"Yes sir. The information is current."

With bottled ink and nibbed pen the old man fashioned the signature which gave the document his blessing. With some relief he removed the pince-nez and sat back.

"Give it a moment to dry." he said pleasantly, not wishing to hurry his company away.

Fleming knew what it was to have an infant family. He chose the morning.

Shortly after nine o'clock, with Ian Pearson, he called at the cottage of Benjamin Kasis. It was Kasis himself who opened the door and Fleming showed him the warrant.

"I should have expected this." Kasis said resignedly.

"You stay with us till we're through." Fleming insisted.

Kasis' wife was busy with the baby and Fleming purposefully left her to her chores. He had already gained an admiration for her as the apartments of the house, unlike that of Masters and Lang, were spotlessly clean. It did not escape his attention that the furnishings were not only clean but mostly new and chosen with great taste. Everything was so neatly in place that searching through drawers and cupboards was embarrassing. Fleming left the embarrassment to Pearson and resorted to leafing through Kasis' telephone and address book, finding all the names and numbers he had expected.

In a bedside drawer Pearson found a half ounce of cannabis and Kasis accepted the find with a grimace.

The men returned to the corridor which ran the length of the house and gave access to the remaining two rooms.

"These rooms are not so tidy." confessed Kasis. "I use them as a workshop."

The police officers soon saw what he meant. The rooms had uncovered stone floors and contained various vehicle parts such as air filters and spotlights but mostly tyres and inner tubes. Fleming spent some time studying the size and condition of the tyres.

"I do my own maintenance." Kasis explained. "Can't afford garages."

"Oh, I don't know," remarked Fleming, "you seem to have been able to buy one or two of your own. Are these compressors, generators, drills and tools all yours?"

"Yeah sure." said Kasis. "Had them for ages."

The last room had a set of stepladders lying against the wall and a collection of plastic sacks piled loosely beside a heap of compost and leaf mould.

"What's all this for?" asked Fleming.

"I'm a gardener." Kasis said blandly.

Fleming looked at the windows of these 'workshop' rooms. The sills were dirty and marked. Obviously materials entered and left by the window.

The men moved back into the corridor without speaking. For Fleming the questions had not been answered. He had found no building society account book and he had found nothing to explain Kasis' ability to make deposits into one. Feeling a little frustrated, he threw his head back and rubbed his chin with his hand. His eyes widened when he realised that he was looking at a trap door in the ceiling. The stepladders no longer seemed so out of place. Fleming remembered the modern skylight windows he had seen from outside the house.

"Ian, bring these steps through."

Pearson reacted by bringing the stepladders. Kasis reacted by groaning.

The police officers climbed to the attic space and invited the gardener to follow them. He did so reluctantly.

The attic was floored and clean but not converted to living accommodation. On two roughly made tables beneath the skylights, plants were being cultivated in large pots. Low voltage heaters were lying beneath the tables.

Fleming looked closely at the plants with their fine stems and long slender leaves. They showed no tendency to be any colour but green. He rubbed his chin again and considered his dilemma. He stood to look quite stupid if he was wrong about the plants and took them away. He would be equally stupid if he left them until he found out what they were and came back to an empty attic.

"I'm taking your plants Mr. Kasis." he announced.

"What for?" Kasis asked in an ominously natural way.

"I think they may be cannabis plants. If they are, the cultivation of them is illegal in this country. They will be examined of course and their type identified but in the meantime I must caution you...."

The plants were confirmed as cannabis plants and Kasis was brought to court. He pled guilty but made the rather predictable claim in mitigation that, as a gardener, he had grown the plants for the challenge of doing so and not for any financial gain. He was told to consider himself fortunate not to be going to prison and he received a £200 fine. This should have placed a strain on his income but he paid the fine in two weeks and the following week Fleming saw him return to the office of the building society, taking money from his pocket as he entered.

The cultivation of cannabis could well have been simply a hobby exercise for the gardener and Fleming was left to contemplate afresh the part being played by Kasis in a much larger scheme, a scheme large enough to provide the sort of financial security he evidently enjoyed.

# SEVEN

It was a beautiful morning and the road was very quiet. Things would become quite different as he drove closer to the city but for the meantime the journey was there to be enjoyed.

Before making this journey, Andy had awaited the return of his photographs from Kevin, with confirmation of Allison's identity as the person in conversation with Manson. It provided enough of a tangible connection that he had requested a meeting with the Detective Superintendent in charge of the Drugs Squad. The time had certainly arrived when he would be wrong to continue to keep all his information to himself.

Kevin had told him of Allison's arrest in Edinburgh. Fleming felt sorry for Kevin. After all the surveillance work he had put in on Allison the arrest had fallen to someone else.

Fleming had also telephoned Colin Goodhew to consolidate what he understood of Cranston. Together they had compared notes and had found that a consistent pattern could be formed from the dates on which the launch had supposedly been hired out to Ricky Walsh by Cranston and the dates marked on Manson's year planner. Colin Goodhew had asked Fleming if he knew a Mr. Delby. It came as news to Fleming that old Freshwater was the owner of a fishing boat in a Welsh boatyard. He had suspected that it might also come as news to Frank 'Freshwater' Delby.

"I can understand what Cranston's up to." Colin had said. "He could not afford to be found hiring out a boat to any subsequent arrested importer. That would be stretching credibility a bit far. So this Delby character is in line to take all the risk of ferrying the stuff himself in a boat that Cranston can claim to have nothing to do with."

Colin had given Andy a considerable list of all boats and vehicles known to be associated with the Cranston Shipping Company. He had also told him of the death of the informer.

"To everyone else it looks like a hit and run road accident. They assume that some drunk driver hit the old guy but for my money, Andy, it was murder. It wouldn't be Cranston himself and I've had a look at the front of the Rolls. It wasn't that vehicle but there are plenty of people working for Cranston who are capable of taking out an informant."

Fleming chose to prefer Colin Goodhew's unsubstantiated version. It was certainly in keeping with all the suspicions he held himself.

The road was becoming busier now but the road down Loch Lomondside was certainly much improved in parts. At times the traffic moved so quickly that no driver could be forgiven for casting admiring glances over the waters of the loch.

Leaving the loch behind and drawing closer to the city Andy Fleming found the traffic heavier and slower, persistently held up by traffic lights and road works. Eventually the journey was reduced to crawling from one set of traffic lights to the next. How could people put up with this sort of carry-on every day?

Despite the delay Andy was in good time for his meeting. Detective Superintendent Lawrence Naismith was also on time. He greeted Andy with a smile and a warm handshake.

The Detective Superintendent had grown up in the west highlands and like many another young man from that part of the world he had come south to gain employment as a police officer in the City of Glasgow. His natural charm and sharp thinking had progressed his career through CID channels and now a greater part of his job was to meet people who could set up operational links and strategy. He lectured to other police officers on the methods used by drug users and couriers, demonstrating the extent of the trafficking problem. He attended elsewhere to listen to the latest accounts of how results were to be achieved. Meeting and greeting people to talk about drugs was what

THE WEED KILLER

Mr. Naismith was good at and he invited Andy to close the room door.

After only a few moments Mr. Naismith could envisage the scope of any enquiry from the range of information available. He stopped Andy Fleming in mid-sentence.

"I'm sorry. I can see that what you have to say is extensive and I think that I should not be the only one to hear it. You would only have to repeat it all, or I would, and it would be better for us not to have to do that. Wait here. I will fetch Mr. Armstrong, the Assistant Chief Constable and Detective Inspector Cooper. Mr. Armstrong is the man to grant expenditure for any operation and Inspector Cooper is the one who has set up previous operations and could be doing so again. Just give me a sec."

Andy did not have to wait long before being introduced to both men and being asked to begin again.

All three men listened intently and Detective Inspector Cooper took notes on a notepad.

When Andy had finished he apologised that his account had not been better prepared but he was assured that everything had been understood.

"What did you make of it, Jim?" asked the Detective Superintendent, turning to his Inspector.

"Sounds very authentic to me." the Inspector replied. "A few of the names mentioned I have noted here. I seem to recognise them. The Edinburgh-Glasgow business of course we already know about. As far as we ourselves are concerned, anything in the remote regions of the West Highlands will cost us. We've had to deal with this before Mr. Armstrong. One or two days is hopeless. One or two men is pointless. Yet to do things properly is extortionate."

It was obviously time to hear from Mr. Armstrong. He was a big surly chap who would always look more like a police officer than an accountant. He paced up and down, rubbing his chin with one hand and pulling his braces out from beneath his jacket with the other. The contrast of the bright red braces with the plain colouring of the other garments brought a smile to Fleming's face. There was enough of a silence that a slight rasping noise could be heard from Mr. Armstrong's chin rubbing.

"This all sounds bad enough to me that I feel we should be doing something Larry." He then turned towards Fleming and continued. "This chap Delby. It could be damn useful to have him working for us. A man on the inside if you like. Would he be the type of man who could be relied on to do that?"

Fleming made a soft groaning sound and shook his head.

"He's a man who scares easily, sir. Not the best sort of nature for a spy. He is in with a crowd who can realistically do more to scare him than we ever could. The only way we might win his confidence is to show that we can deal with him discreetly enough that he could not be discovered by Cranston and company. Take him in from the cold as it were. Bring him here and make him feel important but most of all, make him feel safe. If you fail to make him feel safe he will crack up and become unreliable."

"I get the picture." Mr. Armstrong said grudgingly. "Where he is going to be working it would be someone down there he would need to be in touch with but I still think that we should make the first contact by way of sounding him out."

"Larry, I want you to discuss this whole business with Jim here and with any of the other squads you feel might need to be involved and prepare to draw up a programme of initial investigative study. I shall cost it and I hope to look on it favourably."

"You ought to get the Customs involved here as well at this stage. They probably have a lot of this already. Find out what they are doing or are prepared to do. No reason for us to carry expenditure alone if we can share it with them."

Mr. Armstrong then turned to Andy Fleming.

"You have done well and I realise the amount of self-motivated work you must have put in to have gained all this information but the continuance of such extensive enquiries can be expensive you understand?"

Andy Fleming knew the point only too well.

"Yes sir, I do understand. My phone bill has doubled and my petrol costs are half as much again as they should be. That money has been coming from my own pocket where it was intended for a family that I see less and less of each day. The price of doing extensive enquiries properly is something I do know about."

Mr. Armstrong stepped back, looking slightly gobsmacked.

"Good." he said as nothing else occurred to him.

He had been in headquarters too long to expect a straight talking cop. Headquarters was the home of a bureaucratic structure of men and women who laid out their prayer mats in single file and in the same direction each morning to pass forward romantic gestures of homage.

Here was a man who was different. He spoke face to face, man to man. Quite refreshingly different. Mr. Armstrong smiled and again shook Fleming's hand.

"Nice to have met you." he said quietly. "You have been working very hard. Do not overdo it. Too much voluntary work could bring problems at home."

"Yes sir. I realise that. Thank you."

Detective Superintendent Naismith promised to keep in touch and thanked Fleming for coming down to the city.

The return journey brought a feeling of warm relief. He had shared his burden. He had told his secrets. His suspicions had been accepted as worthy. Leaving the city behind, he entered the God-given splendour of seductive scenery and relaxed to an absorbent pace. The old Vauxhall purred along enjoying a welcome turn of sympathy.

Claas Van Dongen had allowed the telephone to ring for fully five minutes. Still no answer. It was not like Robert Whelan to be unavailable for ten days. The Dutchman was beginning to have feelings of concern for Whelan. If he was honest with himself then he would realise that his concern was not for the well-being of Robert Whelan at all. Whatever befell Whelan would be of no good to the money Van Dongen had invested.

Honesty over the nature of his concern developed into an unease about his invested capital and with cold moist hands Van Dongen rang up his accountants. Feigning calmness, he asked that they make discreet enquiries into the current situation at MacArthur-Whelan Finance.

"What do you mean closed down?"

Cranston's huge fist was in danger of crushing the receiver.

"Nothing left. Just damn-all. Is that what you're telling me? Where's he now?.... ....You don't know. Do you know where my money went?.... ....Oh great. Just bloody great."

The phone was slammed down. Cranston turned away from the telephone and in blind rage punched the door of a highly polished 19th century bureau, creating an ugly split which immediately reduced the value of the item by half.

"Whelan, you bloody weasel, you're dead."

"Mr. Van Dongen?"
The Dutchman looked quizzically at the smartly dressed man with the briefcase and the question.
"Yes. I am Claas Van Dongen. Can I help you?"
"Detective Sergeant Bradshaw, Fraud Squad, Mr. Van Dongen. I hope you can help me. You can perhaps explain your association with the missing Robert Whelan."

It was a dry day but not particularly warm.
Andy Fleming was enjoying the opportunity to patrol alone and on foot. He had made his way along the pier, spending time with the various fishermen and pier hands who had come to know him over recent months.
From the pier he wandered into Donnie Grant's boatyard and was hailed by the genial boat builder from the deck of a small yacht in the corner of the yard. Supported by railway sleepers it was the only vessel to have remained out of the water from the beginning of the season.

"I'll be down in a minute, Andy." Donnie shouted with a smile across his weathered face.

Fleming looked around the yard and gasped as he saw the 'Hand Maiden' tied up at Donnie's small jetty. The cabin door of the boat was open but there was no sign of Manson about the place.

Donnie arrived.

"Boy am I glad for an excuse to leave that job for a minute. It's a gey fiddly affair and my fingers are getting too old and stiff to be annoyed with it. Just like the rest of me."

"There's plenty of life left in your fingers yet," assured Fleming with a smile and he added, "Just like the rest of you."

"What brings you round here today, Andy? Nothing but your usual curiosity no doubt."

"That's right." Fleming agreed. "I was just passing, but now that I am here I am interested as to why that fancy boat is lying at your jetty. She doesn't belong here Donnie. This is clinker country."

"She's not for repair, thank God." said Donnie. "I wasn't here when he brought the boat in but I fancy he has his wife with him for some shopping. I told him a while back that he could use my jetty when he was bringing his wife ashore provided my own jetty was quiet. His wife is scared of climbing up the ladders at the fishing pier. I don't blame her. They can be hellish slippy."

"Have you had a look at the boat?" asked Fleming, nodding towards the 'Hand Maiden'.

"No, not really." replied Donnie. "You know how I feel about fibre glass. I do believe that she's well equipped though." He began to move towards her as he spoke. "She's not my idea of a fishing boat and all that power she has is quite unnecessary."

Stepping aboard the 'Hand Maiden' was straightforward enough but Fleming felt self-conscious.

"What will Manson think if he comes back while we are here?" he asked Donnie.

"That's my workboat on the outside of her. We'll just carry on onto my boat if we see him coming." Donnie assured.

Both men entered the large forward cabin.

"By, somebody's spent a braw penny in here." declared the boat builder. "Look at these instruments. What the hell does he want with all this gear?"

Fleming had seen the navigation before. His interest was elsewhere. He saw that the shelf beside the control switches was stuffed with waterproof clothing and the butt of the shotgun could not be seen. Bending down beneath the level of the control panel he looked through cross members and trailing wires to see the long barrels of the shotgun pointing down towards the junction of the bulkhead with the hull. The weapon had been pushed well down to avoid detection. To retrieve it would still mean pulling it up through the shelf once the waterproof clothing had been removed.

Reaching through towards the bulkhead, Fleming tried to grasp the shotgun and tie it fast using the loose electrical wiring. He could scarcely reach the weapon and succeeded only in pushing the loose wires through the trigger guard.

"What are you doing?" Donnie asked. Fortunately he did not feel inclined to bend down and see for himself.

"Just putting slack wires back into their clip." Fleming answered. "I don't envy any electrician called in to work on this mess."

"Just a typical bloody hippy." Donnie remarked in hopeless disgust. "For all the expensive equipment on board this boat I don't see a single item of safety equipment. No lifejackets, no lifebelts, no flares and no second engine of any sort. Hell mend him if he gets into bother."

They left the vessel and Manson had still not returned.

The supermarket was not exceptionally busy. This was only Wednesday. Things would be different tomorrow afternoon when all the jolly green giro cheques had been cashed. It suited the Mansons to have some space. They hated crowds of normal people. The smaller the crowd the fewer remarks would be passed and the fewer eyes would stare.

Despite such attention they enjoyed these supermarket outings. The delicatessen had such a variety of vegetarian dishes and mixtures and the selection of herbs was fascinating. They studied and discussed everything they saw and the contents slowly building in their trolley were certainly different from most others.

Manson was a creature of instinct and his mind and his eye were tuned to take note of anything unnatural.

For several minutes he had been aware of two men in their twenties and dressed in clean denim whose interest in him seemed unnatural. These men were shopping behind the Mansons and had very few items in their shopping trolley. They seemed to be reluctant shoppers who were finding it difficult to mimic the genuine interest that was delaying the Mansons.

While appearing to talk about shelf goods, Manson informed his wife about these men and they carried on shopping without looking near the men in denim.

The hippy couple finished their shopping at the back of the store and, in marked contrast to their previous pace, they scurried forward to the check-out desks. They smiled at each other in satisfaction as the two denim clad figures arrived hurriedly at check-outs nearer to the main door, their faces anxiously looking to ensure that the Mansons were still in the store.

Manson ordered a taxi to take his groceries back to the boat but then another thought occurred to him. He asked the taxi driver to take him and his wife to the Drypuddle Bar before going to the boatyard.

The thoughts going through Manson's mind were no longer amusing him. He faced the front of the taxi and discouraged his wife from looking back at any following traffic. They returned the driver's pleasantries but said nothing else until the vehicle stopped outside the bar.

"I'll just be a minute." said Manson as he quickly left the taxi and entered the pub.

The bar was empty apart from the barman and by way of explanation Manson mouthed the word 'toilet' as he passed through towards the rear of the premises. Having found the rear door, Manson passed quickly out into the back alley which served several adjoining premises. He ran down the alley until he found a common close through to the street. He walked to the front of the close and glimpsed around the corner of the wall.

As he had suspected, the two men in denims were sitting in a pale blue Cavalier parked down the street from the Drypuddle Bar. The car engine was running and their attention was firmly fixed on the taxi and the front door of the pub. Manson crept back, his face a sombre mask.

The taxi passed Andy Fleming on its way to the boatyard. The policeman waved a half raised hand to the taxi driver but did not betray his recognition of the passengers.

The blue Vauxhall Cavalier followed a few seconds later and the policeman noticed the temptation of the occupants to look at him and nod.

Donnie Grant helped the Mansons to take their polythene bags onto their boat. Manson thanked him and idled the 'Hand Maiden' out from the jetty. Turning her slowly round to head offshore, he looked up to the road above the boatyard. He saw the blue Cavalier parked a short distance beyond the boatyard. The driver had either a camera or binoculars up in front of his face.

There was real venom in the way Manson drew back the throttle lever and threw the 'Hand Maiden' up onto the plane.

From the fishing pier Andy Fleming watched briefly before dipping his head and continuing along the pier. Further along the pier he saw two more young men dressed in denim and standing beside a shed. They seemed to be watching the disappearing 'Hand Maiden' as she headed for Orsaig. Fleming looked at their clean white training shoes, their clean jeans and their white hands. These were no fishermen.

Standing in the mouth of a close some distance from the entrance to the pier, Andy Fleming watched and waited until he saw these two men leave the pier and walk along the Main Street. He followed at a distance

THE WEED KILLER

and saw them enter a close leading to privately owned flats which could be rented on a week by week basis at all times of the year.

Andy walked on past. He knew the man who had the flats, Davie Sneddon, a self employed builder. Before turning down a side street, Fleming looked back in time to see the blue Vauxhall being parked outside the flats. He finished work at six and went home. There was plenty of time to change and eat before going out to watch Fred Lord's cottage.

Since that first Wednesday evening behind the hedge, Fleming had seen the same pattern of behaviour between eight-thirty and nine o'clock each Wednesday. Lord had gone down to the telephone kiosk in preference to his own telephone. This Wednesday Fleming intended to find out why.

Dressed in his customary black, he prepared the small Dictaphone he had borrowed from his father. The sixty minute cassette would be more than enough to capture the conversation, or at least one side of the conversation, provided that Lord spent no more than his usual five or ten minutes on the phone.

Fleming's father had also furnished him with a roll of heavy duty adhesive tape of the type used to bind parcels. All Fleming had required to purchase for the purpose of this operation had been the four new batteries which would ensure optimum performance from the Dictaphone.

Purposefully arriving at the kiosk at eight-fifteen, Fleming unrolled the tape and tore off two ten inch strips. Placing the tape around the pocket Dictaphone he stuck it securely beneath the shelf next to the telephone. He glanced at his watch, almost twenty past eight. He bent down and pressed the red button which began the recording.

Fleming paused briefly to ensure that the mechanism of the machine was not too loud before he left the kiosk and moved stealthily to his vantage point behind the hedge.

Time passed more slowly than usual. Fleming had eyes for only his watch and Fred Lord's door. The door remained closed at eight-thirty and it was still closed at eight-forty.

It was almost eight-fifty before the door opened and Fred Lord appeared. He walked out to the road and turned towards the kiosk. As he looked ahead of him Fred Lord stopped and a look of disgust came over his face.

Fleming looked along to the kiosk and matched Lord's look of disgust. This public telephone in the heart of the country was scarcely used but right now someone was in the kiosk. A red van was parked well back from the kiosk and Fleming could make out from its lettering that it belonged to a local building firm. Some teenage employee had chosen tonight to call a girlfriend from this particular kiosk.

## THE WEED KILLER

Fred Lord walked towards the kiosk and paced to and fro' outside it, looking at his watch. The young man seemed to get the message at once and promptly left the kiosk. Fred Lord went in.

Fleming watched the young man leave and was relieved to see that he did not appear to be carrying anything. It was to be hoped that Lord would also fail to discover the little recording machine.

After a few minutes on the telephone Lord left the kiosk and walked back to his cottage. He seemed to be in a deeply pensive mood.

As soon as Lord entered his house Fleming ran along behind the hedge and across the road to the kiosk. He switched off the recorder and tore it free from the shelf.

In the warmth of his own lounge, with the rest of the household in bed, he settled down to listen to his recording.

He ran the tape fast forward to the halfway point in order to miss the period of inactivity and then rewound slightly to find the sound of a kiosk door opening. He turned the volume up fully and played the tape at normal speed, settling back in his chair to concentrate on every word.

What he heard was sheer filth. Some woman was being asked about her underwear before she hung up. Another two women were called and promised some lewd activity if they were to remove their underwear.

Fleming sighed. Surely this wasn't what he had spent hours watching the cottage for? Could this be the reason for using a telephone away from the cottage? On the tape a door banged and the kiosk fell silent.

Fleming reached forward to switch off the tape but heard the kiosk door open again. After a few seconds the telephone rang.

Fleming stopped, puzzled.

"Bob? It's Fred."

Fleming slapped his leg in annoyance. The boy from the van, of course. How could he have forgotten him? Fleming had simply assumed that the youth had been discouraged from the phone box without making any call. Obviously he had been in the kiosk for several minutes before either Fred Lord or Andy Fleming had seen him. This was Fred Lord's call beginning, a call from someone called Bob.

"Yeah, sure Bob, but what will you do for me?........Okay, but I want it on paper, all legal and watertight........for a while or, ....just a few days is no problem. You could stay with me if you like but you know the risks with that Welsh guy passing the house, or there's Malky, or as a last resort there's always Harry. He could take you anywhere you want to go. .... ....well the offer stands.... It could cost....oh, I see....right then. My name's above the door....yeah sure....good luck...."

Fleming played it over several times. The speech had been quiet but distinct. He had heard every word Fred Lord had said and obviously Bob was being invited to stay on a short visit to the local drugs fraternity but what was to be legal and watertight and who was the Welshman posing a threat? It could be a reference to Norrie Winston but Winston was not actually Welsh. Would Lord know that? Anyway, someone called Bob might be coming to stay.

"Right now," thought Fleming, "it's time for a dram."

He went to the drinks cabinet of the wall unit and poured himself a large malt.

The following morning he breezed into the Police Office more refreshed than usual and found the sergeant studying the incidents from the night before.

"Anything interesting there?" Andy asked.

"Three complaints of dirty phone calls." the sergeant replied with a smile.

"Oh. Give me these to look into." said Fleming. "I think I might get lucky."

The foreign shellfish lorries had been encouraged to park away from residential areas to prevent complaints about their noise and smell.

Fleming knew well enough where these lorries had been in the habit of parking and he drove around town checking the out-of-the-way parking areas. Drivers arrived late and left early. They were forced to park in out-of-the-way places and, because the tourists had accounted for all accommodation, the drivers slept in their cabins. Parking of lorries, even fish lorries, on the piers during the night was strictly forbidden.

At last Fleming found the lorry he had been looking for. A large white juggernaut with hardly a word of English on it. At the top of the windscreen a cartoon sticker of a smiling duck with a French flag identified the lorry as the one used by Winston. The curtains were already drawn around the cabin windows but through them Fleming could see the soft flickering glow of a portable black and white television screen.

The arrival of the lorry was expected.

Andy Fleming had kept careful note of the previous arrival dates for these lorries and he had studied them in conjunction with the dates given to him by Colin Goodhew for Walsh's use of Cranston's boat and the dates that he himself had noted from Manson's year planner diary. He knew that there would be no Customs men on the pier in the morning when the lorry went to collect Manson's shellfish.

Fleming knew this because he had been there himself on previous occasions but he had not witnessed the exchange of anything but shellfish and hard cash. Only by keeping up his surveillance could he hope to establish how the transfer of the cannabis was being done.

Shortly before seven o'clock the following morning Fleming parked his old Vauxhall in the main street and entered a close between two shops. He climbed the common staircase to the first floor and looked out from the window at the front of the landing. He raised the powerful binoculars that a thoughtful Mary had purchased for him at Christmas and he surveyed the pier.

The large white lorry was parked near the edge of the pier and the driver was syphoning sea water into his tanks by means of a pump. The pump was powered by a small generator.

The lorry driver was not alone for he had been joined by Norrie Winston. Both men strode around the lorry, apparently managing some sort of conversation, while they awaited the arrival of the 'Hand Maiden'.

Fleming scanned the waters beyond the pier in search of Manson and eventually saw him a good way off. He seemed to be approaching from the ferry point on the shore road and not from Orsaig as Fleming had expected.

Fleming watched the operation as he had done on so many previous mornings. There seemed to be very few people about at the moment but there had been mornings when groups of tourists had stood and watched everything the men did. Some had come forward to examine the shellfish. Some had asked questions and several photographs had been taken. It had never seemed to bother Winston in the way Fleming would have expected if any part of a drugs transfer was taking place.

Even this morning, with virtually nobody about, the shellfish were being landed in an overt and natural way. He concentrated hard on every blue plastic basket of shellfish as it was lifted onto the pier by Manson. He saw the foreign lorry driver weigh each basket and he saw Norrie Winston write down the weight of each basket before the lorry driver took it into the rear of the lorry, returning seconds later with the empty basket. When the consignment had been transferred in this way Winston was in conversation with Manson but the men never approached each other. Manson raised his hand for the money he was being given but that remained the closest and only contact. Just like before.

If Fleming had not been concentrating on the activity on the pier he might have noticed the yellow van which drove into town from the coast road and turned south to the junction of the back road which led into the country.

Kasis stopped near the junction and looked anxiously about him. Where was this man he was supposed to pick up? Why wasn't he here waiting? He had no wish to be lingering anywhere with his load of bagged peat and leaf mould. It looked innocent enough but he would continue to feel vulnerable until he had joined Winston and the lorry and got rid of it. He had orders to pick up a passenger this morning and take him to Winston along with the bags, but there was nobody here. Kasis didn't feel much like waiting for anyone.

As the driver and Winston boarded their lorry Manson turned the 'Hand Maiden' away from the pier and Fleming lowered his binoculars. Looking towards the entrance to the pier Fleming saw a group of three men who had not been there earlier.

He raised his binoculars again and scarcely believed what he saw. Two of the denim clad officers were walking to a third man close to the entrance to the pier. The third man seemed ill at ease and moved away from them with his arms spread out and his face a mask of protest.

Fleming could well understand why Frank Delby would be worried. Matters were not about to improve for him either as the large white juggernaut passed on its exit from the pier. If Delby failed to see Winston then Norrie Winston had certainly not failed to see him. With the lorry now driving towards him on the main street Fleming could see Winston studying the large rear view mirror on his cab door. As he looked back Winston was obviously angry and Fleming could almost hear the obscenities he saw being mouthed.

The lorry continued on its way and Fleming looked back towards the pier entrance.

Freshwater was walking smartly away from the other two men. The drug squad officers looked at each other with expressions of disappointment. Fleming's expression was more akin to Winston's. Fleming ran to his old Vauxhall and drove off towards the block of flats in the cul-de-sac. He should have arrived before Delby but Frank Delby never did arrive. Andy hurried home to change into his uniform in order to begin his shift at nine o'clock. As he was about to leave, Mary called him back.

"Andrew, telephone....it's for you."

Fleming took the handset from the small table.

"Yes."

"I'm done for man. I'm as good as dead right now." The voice was high-pitched and scared. It was Frank Delby.

"Calm down Frank. How do you mean you're dead? What happened?"

"I was going with them this morning. I was going south to the job. I would've phoned you when I got the chance but your guys picked me up when I was waiting for my lift. They wanted me to keep them in touch with what was happening, well I can tell you what's happening Andy, I'm going man. I'm going where no bugger can find me. I don't need the hassle. I'm gone man, understand? Out of sight."

"Wait a minute Frank. Where are...."

## THE WEED KILLER

It was pointless to say more. The handset now produced a quiet Brrrrrr-ing sound. Fleming replaced the handset and headed for the old Vauxhall.

When he reached the office Fleming phoned Colin Goodhew and told him what had happened.

"I don't hold out much hope, Colin, but let me know if he shows up at your end."

"All right, Andy. I'll keep watching the boatyard but like yourself I'm not too hopeful."

# EIGHT

Frank Delby considered himself fortunate to have found a lorry driver prepared to give him a lift south.

It seemed like hours that he had spent walking along the side of the road, raising his thumb hopefully as each vehicle passed. The day had been pleasant enough but the breeze from the steady flow of traffic had made Frank feel cold.

It may not have been the breeze alone which had chilled him. In his mind he was confused as to what he should do and where he should go but in his heart he was scared, scared that nowhere would provide safe refuge for him. Whatever the reasons, he had been chilled to the bone by the time the wood lorry had stopped for him.

The cabin smelled of spent oil and his seat jumped and swayed enough to make rolling his cigarette an extremely awkward job. For the time being he felt safer. The warmth was beginning to return to his fingers and the cigarette might yet be complete.

## THE WEED KILLER

The middle aged driver looked across at his passenger and glanced at the fumbling hands which were trying to trap loose tobacco in a small scrap of white paper. He threw Delby a sympathetic smile before returning his attention to the road ahead.

Delby could not make up his mind where he wanted to go to escape the wrath of Norrie Winston. He had always fancied a spell on the north coast of France. He had known a mate once who had worked there over a winter and had enjoyed it. Perhaps this was the time to try it.

At last the cigarette was finished. He stuck it in his mouth and tidied up his tobacco box. The driver looked across with a smile and shouted above the engine noise, "You made it."

Delby did not feel like shouting. He simply put up a thumb and winked.

Drawing deeply on the cigarette, he reflected on the events which had brought him to this flight south.

Norrie Winston had hardly seemed to pay him any attention when Winston first arrived to work on the coaster. While others had listened to Delby's humorous anecdotes, Winston had always ignored him.

The day had finally arrived when Winston had spoken to him. By then Winston had learned that among the crew Delby was the one he was looking for, a single man, a loner but a good seaman. Frank had been told that he could earn good money by just running a small boat with the occasional job for a friend of Winston's. The money he was to be paid by Winston's friend would provide a guaranteed income and any other work would be his own affair. The deal had sounded good and the restless Delby was in the mood for a change from the coaster at that time. Only after the agreement had been struck had it occurred to Delby that there might be drugs involved. Winston continually referred to the deal that they had made and warned him to talk to no-one about it. If he opened his mouth about it then his mouth would be closed permanently. "Just do the job and take the money" had been Winston's advice.

He had been afraid of Winston then and he still was. That cop, Andy Fleming, had sounded like he understood the problem and had promised to help. He was going to get the professionals to look after Delby. "Don't worry Freshwater," he had said, "you'll be in good hands."

Some good hands they had turned out to be.

Winston had said, "Seven o'clock mind, don't be late. A guy in a van will pick you up and bring you to me. I'll take you to where the job is. If you're not there on time the guy won't wait and I'll be looking for ya."

Delby shivered as he remembered the way Winston had said this. The lorry driver looked across and shouted, "Still cold?" Delby shook his head and raised a thumb. "I'm fine." he said loudly. He turned towards the window and his mind projected memories of its own onto the darkness outside.

He had been in good time. He had been early by ten minutes. These guys in the Vauxhall had fooled him.

"You Frank Delby?"

"Aye. I'm Delby."

"Get in."

What else could he do? Okay it wasn't one guy, it was two guys. It wasn't a van, it was a blue Vauxhall car. How many folk would know him by name at ten to seven in the morning and stop to offer him a lift.

By the time he knew the answers to his questions the Vauxhall was half a mile from the pick-up point passing the entrance to the pier.

"Drug Squad? Oh great, just great. I was waiting for a lift, now I've missed it. Let me out. Let me out right now."

When they had stopped he had got out but they had got out as well. They had tried to talk with him as he walked backwards, raising his arms in protest.

Would he keep them informed? These guys were not for real. They didn't look much now like the safe hands that Fleming had referred to.

He had run back to the junction and waited. He was late. No van ever came. He had taken a bus for as far as his money would allow, just to get away from the place. This had left him with forty-five pence and less than quarter of an ounce of tobacco. He had spent twenty pence phoning Fleming before heading off on foot.

The wood lorry driver had promised to take him as far as the most southerly service station on his route. That should give Delby a fair chance of finding a lorry to take him on to the south coast.

Frank nicked his cigarette and put the remaining portion in his jacket pocket. The warmth of the cab had relaxed him. His head rolled onto his shoulder and he fell asleep.

The driver looked across and smiled. He knew that a man had to be pretty tired before he could fall asleep in this lorry. As the miles passed relentlessly Delby turned, stretched, twitched and groaned but never woke. With a jerky, rocking motion and a loud hiss the lorry eventually came to rest.

"Hey sir. Wake up."

Delby awoke with a start. It was dark. The lorry was stopped. He glanced outside. There seemed to be hundreds of other lorries parked in rows.

"Here you are old son," the lorry driver said jovially, "the end of the line. I'm not going in here but if you go in for a bite to eat and ask around you'll find a driver to take you south."

"Right, right." said Delby, slowly remembering what his intentions had been. "Thanks a million, man. Sorry I dropped off on you."

Delby jumped down and returned the driver's wave before slamming the cab door. He shivered a little as the heavy wood lorry roared away towards the motorway. The evening air was cool.

He walked over to the windows of the cafe and looked in at the many tables inside, all busy with drivers of one sort or another. He felt hungry but with twenty five pence in his pocket he would have to stay that way. He wandered off to the line of parked lorries and looked at each one in turn, considering the home base printed on the cab doors. He had been wondering how he might get across to France and here was a lucky break, a big white foreign lorry. He lit up his cigarette butt and stamped his feet as he waited for the lorry driver to come back to the lorry. His cigarette smoke drifted upwards past the smiling face of a French duck.

It seemed like ages since Andy Fleming had gone out to relax over a pint of beer. The extensive hours and the lack of cash had left no real opportunity for socialising in any way. Now that four other officers were running about the place and keeping an eye on things, surely he could manage to take a break. He had no desire to tread on their toes, after all, he was not supposed to know they were there.

Mary could scarcely afford to give him any money for a drink but she seemed to realise that he had placed himself under considerable strain. If a night out would help him to relax it might mark the beginning to a more normal existence and she was all for that.

Sitting back in the quiet lounge bar with his pint of Guinness in front of him and an artificial coal fire off to his right, Andy Fleming felt relaxed. So relaxed did he feel that he was worried about falling asleep.

In days past he had enjoyed meeting up with members of the criminal fraternity for a quiet pint. When he was not at work and they were not in prison it had always provided a stimulating challenge to joust with slightly impaired intellects. He had no wish to meet any such person tonight. He doubted if he had the stamina for a conversation and had chosen the quietest lounge quite deliberately.

As he dozed over his second pint he was joined by someone who was certainly not of the criminal fraternity, or any other fraternity.

The shapely form of Loretta MacAuley settled beside him and she blew softly into his ear. He awoke with a start.

He had become friends with Loretta and her boyfriend, David Russell. Davy Russell was a sullen type who spoke to Fleming but would tell him nothing.

The two men got on well together nevertheless and Loretta shared David's respect for the police officer. Whenever she had consumed a few vodkas she was inclined to admit to feeling more than respect but Andy was not given to encouraging her.

"Hello doll. How are you?"

"Oh, can't complain Andy. You're a big stranger. God, it's been ages since I saw you in here. You're looking well mind you."

The couple chatted and drank quietly together and Andy Fleming became glad of the company he had. Nobody who knew Loretta could seriously consider that her being with Andy Fleming had any scandalous overtones. She was regularly playing companion to her friends but her reputation was intact.

She leaned towards Andy and spoke quietly.

"Davy was saying that the Drugs boys were up here. They are watching that guy on Orsaig apparently."

Fleming could hardly feel surprised at Loretta hearing this. From what he had seen himself half the town must know what was going on, particularly those involved in drugs.

"I don't really know about them, Loretta. Nothing gets said. You know what I mean?"

Undeterred, Loretta continued.

"Davy says that the guy is worth watching. He is friendly with that Felton Lang and Benjamin Kasis. Lang takes drugs to Edinburgh and Kasis goes to Perth, Inverness and Aberdeen."

Andy Fleming was interested in this information, even if it was second hand, for it supported what he already knew. Not that Davy Russell would have approved.

"That guy on Orsaig, Manson, he gets the stuff from a deep sea trawler. Davy reckons it must be one of these Welsh or Jersey boats but he says that these Drug Squad guys won't catch Manson."

"Davy's probably right." said Andy, hoping to give Loretta the impression that he knew less about Manson than she did.

"That Manson guy is mixed up with some real bad people. Davy says that that Norrie Winston is one of them. The local fishermen won't talk Andy, but they are scared, shit scared. Davy knows there's trouble brewing. Felton Lang told him that some guy has let them all down and now anything could happen. This bugger that made off with the money, he's as good as dead apparently."

They left before closing time and Andy walked Loretta home. Not that she needed protection, not in this area. If nothing else, the West Highlands had not yet become a high risk area for crime against the innocent.

The evening had been cordial and relaxing. Loretta was pleasant and beautiful company, if something of a wild card. Andy tried to convince her that she should marry Davy Russell and settle down.

"I would hate to see you still in this dithering state in ten years time, kid. Fifteen years ago I would have married you myself but now nothing would please me more than seeing you and Davy get hitched."

"Do you think that we could have an evening like this together if I was married to Davy?" she teased.

"Of course. He would still be fishing, wouldn't he? Naturally I would ask his permission." Andy kidded.

They laughed and Loretta squeezed his arm.

When they reached the close leading to Loretta's flat they said their 'Good nights' and Loretta gave him the customary peck on the cheek. It was a pleasant end to a pleasant evening which had not promised or promoted anything beyond the existing, teasing friendship.

Andy made his way back to the town centre, passing the blue Vauxhall parked outside the builder's flats. He looked up and saw the lighted window.

"You won't learn much up there, boys." he chuckled to himself.

Claas Van Dongen had not enjoyed his conversation with Detective Sergeant Bradshaw. It was quite obvious that Robert Whelan had made off with everyone else's money, including Van Dongen's. Computerised transfer had allowed this to happen spontaneously and before the subscribers had realised. So blatant was the removal that Whelan was assumed to have skipped the country. Van Dongen had no ideas to offer Bradshaw as to where his one-time friend might have gone. He had been at pains to play down the 'friend' description used by Bradshaw. It had been a business relationship, pure and simple and now they could never be friends.

For several days the Dutchman did nothing about the matter. For the first time in his life he felt diffident, stupid and edgy. He had hoped that Whelan would phone to explain himself or that the bank manager would call to say that the money was back in place. Van Dongen had been careful not to give MacArthur Whelan Finance enough to break him but, for the time being, a little colour had drained from the face of capitalism.

Like a mourner coming to terms with a death, he began to think of putting his house back in order. The visit of David Bradshaw had frightened him and he was no longer prepared to involve himself with the drugs trade, not even at a distance.

Reaching into the inside pocket of an unused sports jacket he took out an old diary. The 'Notes' page held several entries written at different times and different angles but he found 'Flashmore' and the number he wanted.

"Harry. Claas Van Dongen here."

"Yes Mr. Van Dongen, what's the problem?"

Manson was sure that there must be a problem. Van Dongen had not been in the habit of calling him on the phone and he never before referred to him as Harry.

"There has been a financial crisis, Harry. I am sorry for you but the business cannot continue. You can sell the boat if you can find a buyer but I would want at least twenty-five thousand, you understand. If you can get that amount then you can get five thousand for yourself. It will help you towards a fresh start."

"How soon would you want this done?" asked Manson unhappily.

"Oh within the next month or six weeks I think. After that I would not expect the market to remain favourable to the sale of fishing boats."

"The boat is well insured Mr. Van Dongen. Why not sink her for the insurance? I could arrange that no bother at all." Manson suggested with visions of a bigger reward than the five thousand presently on offer.

"No. I think that is a bad idea, Harry. It would be very obvious and suspicious and one investigation could lead to another."

"All right." Manson agreed. "I'll ask around and let you know how I get on. I suppose I'll have to give up the lease of the cottage here?"

"No. It doesn't cost that much at all. If you are happy there I will continue to pay your rent."

Van Dongen was pleased to be able to finish on a generous note. He had avoided explanations and if Manson did not know the state of affairs with Whelan then he could not talk to others about it. These were dangerous times.

Fleming crawled over the frosted ground towards the cottage. Now that the leaves were leaving the trees it was necessary to arrive in darkness as the skeletonised undergrowth could no longer provide cover. It was six in the morning and Fleming hoped that he was the only person inclined to have open eyes at that early hour.

Felton Lang's yellow van had been returned by Kasis and beside it sat a red Renault car. With unfeeling fingers Andy reached into his pocket and withdrew a small notebook and pencil. He quickly noted the number of the Renault car and replaced his notebook. He crept forward and looked into the back of the yellow van and saw that it contained only the spare wheel and tyre. Being careful not to leave obvious footprints he began the half mile walk to his own vehicle.

Once home he rang his office and asked that the ownership of the red Renault be given to him. He recognised the name and address as one he had received from Kevin. The visitor to Lang's home was one of Allison's henchmen from Aberdeen.

"So it's business as usual." Fleming thought to himself as he ran the hot bath he hoped would revive him.

The children had left for school and Mary was stuffing her washing machine. Andy was under no obligation to hurry through his bathing. He soaked in the warm, soapy water and his body tingled in gratitude. It would not matter to him if he never had to leave the bath but he suspected that his bliss might be short-lived when he heard Mary answer the telephone.

She tapped on the bathroom door.

"Andy. It's Superintendent Naismith for you."

Fleming rose quickly from the bath and threw a bath towel around himself. He did not want the expense of returning the call.

"Yes sir. Good morning. You have caught me in the bath I'm afraid."

"Sorry about that." the Superintendent apologised. "I just wanted to tell you that I had a team of boys up beside you for the last few days. They're back now."

"Yes, I know." Fleming replied with some satisfaction. "Four men in a blue Vauxhall and staying in one of Davy Sneddon's flats."

"There's not much gets by you." the Superintendent laughed. "They have brought back scores of photographs of people and vehicles they found interesting and suspicious. They have little stories to tell about the people they photographed and I would like you to look in the next time you're down and help out with some of the identification."

There was something ominously uninspired about the way Naismith had said 'look in the next time you're down'. No rush and no urgency were all too often symptomatic of no interest.

"Yeah sure sir. I'll do that. What about the matter of an operation and the Customs, what have they got planned?" Fleming pressed. He had been disappointed that such things had not been the reason for the Superintendent's phone call.

"Well the operational side of things is being handed over to the Scottish Crime Squad. They have better facilities and procedures for the crossing of regional and national boundaries. As for the Customs, they are concentrating their efforts on the Welsh coast. They see this man Cranston as the driving force and they are determined to nail him. It might be that they force him further north and you could see this man Manson getting a bit busier."

"Hard to tell how busy he is." Fleming remarked. "I see him landing shellfish but I don't see him landing drugs. I'm sure he is landing the stuff though and I'm equally sure that one way or another these big lorries are taking it south. Surely between the Customs and ourselves we could have them stopped somewhere and searched. Somewhere on the road south. Somewhere well away from here but well short of any likely dropping off point."

"Better still if they simply followed them and got the whole picture but that's a matter for the Crime Squad boys." Larry Naismith said plainly. "But on the subject of these lorries. One of them was hi-jacked in France. We got a copy of the telex that Interpol sent. The driver had that chap Winston with him. They claimed to have been robbed of thirty-five thousand pounds or perhaps the equivalent in francs. The proceeds of shellfish sales they say."

"It might surprise you what the French are prepared to pay for their shellfish you know." Fleming said informedly. "Fifteen pounds per pound for some of it.

THE WEED KILLER

I don't see the advantage of reporting such a robbery. Surely they would never get insurance cover for the loose cash they carry about with them?"

"No. I wouldn't have thought so either." agreed Larry Naismith. "Perhaps he is looking for a way to explain to his bank manager the hole which recently appeared in his bank balance."

"You mean the loss he took when Walsh was arrested?" Fleming asked.

"Yes. I think thirty-five thousand might have been about the sort of figure involved there. By the way, the boys spoke to your friend Delby. I don't think he is going to play ball."

"I can't say that I blame him." Fleming remarked with a heavy hint of disgust.

"How's that?" Naismith said warily.

"I'm afraid your men took him away from a meet with the bad guys and spoke to him right under Norrie Winston's nose. I doubt if the poor bugger will get Walsh's job now. He'll be lucky to get away with his life."

"Oh well. As you say, not too surprising we lost that one." Naismith said with a sigh.

It was Fleming who kept the conversation alive.

"By the way. Felton Lang is still in business with Aberdeen. He has had one of Allison's cronies down staying with him."

"That's typical I suppose." remarked the Superintendent. "Getting the ringleader stops things for the moment but not for too long. I could even believe that Allison is running things from his prison cell. Difficult to kill off these guys completely."

"Maybe," said Fleming, "but we hardly amount to a lethal dose of prevention."

"I suppose not." conceded Larry Naismith. "But you hang in there and let us know of anything significant that crops up. You will have to be our eyes and ears for a while longer. Nobody could do it better."

"Right sir," said Fleming, "and I won't forget to look by some day and explain your photograph album to you. In the meantime I'm heading for hypothermia. Thanks for phoning. I'll be in touch."

Fleming ran more water and slipped back into his bath. He again enjoyed the warmth of the water but struggled to resist an urge to punch a hole in the bathroom wall.

"Just keep going Andy. You're doing a good job, Andy. You're the best Andy. And why? You're the cheapest form of labour we have, Andy. Those of us in timeshare suits don't have the money or the inclination to do anything but sit around drinking coffee and talking about the way we destroy potential informants."

Fleming held his breath and let his head slip below the water. His head needed cooling. He could feel the rage building inside him as he thought of the money being spent on anti-drugs campaigns and the promise of politicians and chief police officers that all was being done to combat the drugs menace. He thought of the crazy sixteen year old kid he had locked up for causing hundreds of pounds worth of damage while stoned out of his mind. He recalled how he had watched the same kid at nineteen being carried off to the mortuary after overdosing on drugs at a party. He could still see the kid's face as clearly as he could remember the face of young Stevie. Who was really trying to stop this madness by eliminating the importers and dealers? Were Colin and Kevin the only people who shared his wish to stop the misery, to cut to the action without all this inconsequential posturing?

He could remember the sort of remarks which had been passed when he had left to come to the highlands. Of how the heather would soon be in his ears and how the man was going out to the sticks in search of early retirement.

He knew why he had left. His reasons were probably the same as others who had left busier, more crowded places to come to this tranquil splendour. Perhaps they had become disenchanted with the attempts of professional people to hold society together. Political correctness had become cancerous, destroying and replacing honest sense, and good men had thrown in the towel. Perhaps by leaving he had become one who had thrown in the towel himself. He could be forgiven for giving up but he had made himself a promise, a promise he had not yet kept.

There was something of a new beginning in the way the highland community life suited all who came to it. The doctor was not a doctor treating patients because that was his job. He was a man who did not want his friend to be ill and was privileged to help. The teacher was able to teach classes of such a size that each child received tuition as an individual. Funerals and weddings were not things that constantly happened to other people, they were something happening to someone you knew. How could anyone hold the impression that this was not real living? There was much for the city slicker to learn in the highlands but only when he came to realise that, could he learn the lesson.

As the bath water cooled, so did Fleming. There were plenty of people out there who wanted the drugs barons caught. There had to be. Why else would these political heads spout forth such sense before failing to shape up?

As he rubbed himself down violently with a warm towel, Fleming realised that he was still a man of conviction whose mission was not yet over.

Harry Manson and his wife had discussed their predicament at length and had come up with no real answers.

They had lived well and easily from their part in the drugs routes managed by Cranston and funded by Whelan. Fishing had become little more than a hobby to turn to between drops from the 'Moon Vixen'. If these drops were to stop, Harry Manson would have to return to fishing for real and he could expect precious little in return for his type of effort. He would have to begin by spending the five grand from Van Dongen on a fishing boat. That much money would not buy much of a boat and after the 'Hand Maiden' anything less would be hard to live with.

He rolled a joint and passed it over to his wife before starting one for himself.

"At least we have the roof for a while," Manson said consolingly, "and the hens will keep laying."

"I'm not into eggs man, you know that." his wife reminded him. She was strictly vegetarian and that meant no eggs. "If you live on nothing but eggs you could turn into one."

"Don't mind a bit. Not if it helps me get laid." He chuckled and lit his joint.

The telephone rang and Manson looked at his wife with a puzzled expression on his face before reaching for the telephone handset.

"Hello."

"Is that you Manson? 'Garth' Cranston here." The voice was loud and the manner overbearing. Cranston always called himself 'Garth' when he felt that a reminder of his size would be an advantage. "Have you seen anything of that bastard, Whelan?"

"No. I can't say I have." Manson spoke honestly.

"Well, listen Manson, I want that bastard dead. He's done a runner with my money and nobody does that and lives, you hear, nobody."

Cranston was venting his rage and Manson's wife could hear his every word from where she sat.

"It's got nothing to do with me, man. I'm all through here. I gotta sell the boat and then I'm finished." Manson explained.

"So the Dutchman's giving up." Cranston said in a quieter, more considerate tone. He even remained silent for a second or two before resuming in acceptable volume. "You can still work for me. Move north. Somewhere on the mainland where that mate of yours, Ewan Brunton, can get to you. You could meet the lorry. You'll get a fair shake from me, you know that. What do you say?"

"Sounds fine to me." Manson agreed. "I'll speak to the wife and we'll get organised. Is there a number I can get you at?"

"No." said Cranston emphatically. "You tell Norrie Winston anything you have to tell me. If you see that weasel Whelan, you tell Winston about it you hear. I want Whelan dead. I've got five grand waiting for the man that gets him. No bastard crosses Cranston and lives. A hundred for you Manson if you see him, five grand if you kill him."

"Sure man, sure, and thanks a lot. I'm gone."

## THE WEED KILLER

Manson felt better, a lot better. He drew deeply on his joint. Whelan would never show up on Orsaig. He would be on the other side of the world by now.

"We're moving to a new roof kid." he told his wife smoothly. "We're sharing Ewan's scene and we're back in business."

She smiled in relief.

Manson studied his wife's thin legs as they stretched down from the straw basket chair on which she was perched. She was like a hen in a skirt, but while cannabis did nothing for his perception of a hen it seemed to work for his perception of her.

"You know kid, I got that egg feeling coming on." he mused.

The lounge was small and the lighting was subdued. Soft orchestral music prevented silence. The handful of patrons either spoke in whispers or not at all. The hotel was discreet and anonymous. It did not bother Whelan that he could not remember the name of the place.

He stared at the glass of brandy in front of him on the dark oak table and thought of his lifelong struggle to live in some style.

His earliest days had been spent in Ireland where his mother had gone with her drunkard husband. They must have married, he supposed, for he had his father's name but he could no more remember his father than he could recall the little house in Monaghan.

His mother had brought him back to Glasgow and they had stayed in a single room but not for long. The war had meant work for his mother and young Robert Whelan had been sent to stay with 'Granny MacArthur' on the Isle of Skye.

She had been good to him and on the day he had left her to go south she had given him his birth certificate. He had kept the document a safe secret ever since. His whole life had been spent as Robert Whelan the master planner of fraudulent schemes, of his own fortune and of his own future. In Ireland his fortune awaited and in America his future.

He looked down at the briefcase at his feet. It was too valuable to leave in any hotel room. He reached into his inside pocket and took out his passport. He had never used it before but the photograph was a current likeness. From his wallet he took out his birth certificate and smiled down at it. In a couple of days he would be a new man beginning a new life.

He had earned the opportunity, he would have argued.

He had organised the importation through the Cranston Shipping Company. He had arranged a respectable stepping stone ashore by convincing the reputable Claas Van Dongen to provide a local fishing boat and skipper. He had harnessed the large juggernaut lorries which ran conveniently from isolated spots on the Scottish west coast to the main market targets in the south on routes appropriate to their legitimate trade. From these southerly bases Whelan had set up the nationwide network which supplied everything from top night clubs to large deprived housing estates, even ensuring that sufficient quantities returned north to meet Scottish demand. Van Dongen was right. Drugs were a filthy business but they had provided a gravy train to wealth. Whelan had ridden the train long enough and now he was stepping off.

He raised the brandy glass to his lips and looked over it at the attractive lady sitting alone and paying more attention to him with each large gin.

At seven-thirty the next morning an Audi sped away from the quiet hotel and headed for the Scottish border. Whelan had paid his bill and had been careful to leave nothing in his room except a sleeping beauty with a fondness for gin. It did not matter to him that he had never known her name.

# NINE

It was seven o'clock in the morning and Fleming had just returned from an unremarkable tour of estate cottages, car parks and waterside venues.

He switched on the kettle and sat down to pull off his Wellington boots. Mary had heard him coming in and she staggered through from the bedroom, yawning lengthily. She jumped as the telephone rang on the hall table and for once her husband beat her to it.

"Hello."

"Hello. Is that an Andrew Fleming?"

"Yes."

"This is a Chief Inspector Hollis of the police at Northampton. I have been given your name and address by the Post Office. I have your telephone number in front of me on a scrap of paper and it is the only clue I have to help me identify someone we found on the M1 this morning. Have you any friends or relatives down this way?"

"No. I don't know anyone as far south as that except the odd police officer who might have my telephone number. I am actually a police officer myself. What has this person done?"

"Oh I see. You are a police officer but this is your home telephone number?" the Chief Inspector said slowly.

"Yes. That's right. Is there a problem with this person you have? Can he not explain to you why he has my home telephone number?" Fleming asked as he began to wonder if the call was genuine or some sort of inquisitive hoaxer.

"The man I have is dead, Mr. Fleming. Judging by his appearance I would say it is unlikely that he is a police officer. He was lying on the motorway and I doubt if he has a whole bone in his body. All he has on him is twenty-five pence, a tobacco tin and this piece of paper with your telephone number. Have you any ideas as to who he is?"

"Yes." said Fleming with a sigh. "I think he might be Francis 'Freshwater' Delby. Freshwater is a nickname. He is on file and has several distinguishing features. You should find him on computer all right. You'll see from his record that he gets around. He has no next of kin that I know of. He has been up here recently and phoned me the morning before last. He phoned me at home. I'm in the book but he's obviously noted my number for some reason."

There was a pause while the Chief Inspector noted down the name of Francis Freshwater Delby and considered what had been said.

"Why did he phone you?" the Chief Inspector asked. It was the type of formal questioning that Fleming detested so much.

"To say that he was going away." Fleming said plainly.

"Why should he do that? I mean to phone you at home like that? He is a convicted criminal isn't he?"

"When you see his record," Fleming said wearily, "you will notice that I have a case pending against this man. He had promised to let me know if he was moving on. He would know that I was off-duty but criminal or not he kept his promise. I would be able to identify the man formally if that would help. Now how did he die?"

"It looks like he wandered onto the motorway and got struck by a vehicle, or maybe by several vehicles." the Chief Inspector said nonchalantly.

"Yeah. You're probably right, Chief Inspector." Fleming said with a despairing shake of the head. Presumably this would be the last occasion when the police could treat Freshwater's welfare with nonchalance.

Fleming prepared for work. He would phone Colin from the office.

The morning was comfortably warm and Constable Fleming had chosen a spot in the sun to watch over the whole street as it buzzed in Friday fashion to bring the business week to a close.

## THE WEED KILLER

As his gaze took in The Fred Lord Shop with its display windows lit to best effect for the enticement of the jewellery conscious tourist his mouth twisted in annoyance. Parked at the kerb was a new Ford Granada, the property of Fred Lord and a dramatic improvement on the old Cortina. How galling it seemed to Fleming that only two years had passed since this man had earned a living from fitting worktops and window catches in otherwise complete houses. Was no-one entitled to ask how this had happened? Bill Maitland, the bank manager, had remarked to Fleming once on the remarkable rise in fortunes of this particular man but the law itself had prevented any true disclosure of what Mr. Maitland knew. While Andy Fleming had acknowledged and appreciated the innuendous remarks of Mr. Maitland, a court of law would never admit them to be heard.

As he recalled the disappointment of some recent sentences he had seen in the newspapers Fleming noticed two men emerge from The Fred Lord Shop.

One was Fred Lord himself and the other was an older man. This other man was tall, erect, well-groomed and a gentleman with the bearing of a military or naval officer. He wore a sheepskin jacket and carried a briefcase.

The two men exchanged a few words and a handshake at the door of the shop before the tall gent strode off down the street. Fred Lord returned to his shop.

Constable Fleming watched the man in the sheepskin jacket and wondered if he had been a salesman, an accountant or perhaps a customer. A puzzled look came over the police officer's face as he saw the gentleman step into a taxi further down the street. The taxi drove past Fleming and the distinguished looking passenger gave Fleming a cold stare.

Only a few moments later Fred Lord came from his shop carrying a cardboard folder and drove off, in his Granada, in the opposite direction.

Manson's telephone had never been as busy. Now it rang again.

"Hello….hey Malky my man. What gives?"

The fisherman listened to what Malcolm Masters had to say and his body stiffened. His jaw dropped and his heart sank a little.

"So he's staying with you. Did you have to tell me man? I don't want to know the guy. Why tell me?"

As Manson listened further he began to wish that he had never answered the telephone.

"He wants me to take him? You know what you are asking man? You could get me killed here. You know that?"

Manson began to shuffle and fidget. He just did not want to be involved.

"Hey I don't know man. This is kinda heavy….oh, bread, sure. Bread will be real useful when I'm dead….

how much? It would have to be up front man, you tell him that."

Sunday mornings have a reputation for being respectfully uneventful in the west highlands but they also have a habit of producing something to interest the local constabulary.

John Grierson headed out by Land Rover to investigate a call from a group of teenage boys who had broken the Sabbath to drive around the cliff tops north of the town on their trial bikes. The boys had discovered a car lying upside down in the water at the base of the cliff.

Constable Grierson looked down at the upturned car with sea water lapping around its sides. The boys told him that when they had first seen it the water had been lapping over the vehicle. The tide was going out.

The officer began to pick his way down the cliff. There was no need to hurry. The longer he took, the farther out the tide would go, leaving the car much easier to examine.

By the time he reached the vehicle he was able to walk around it and over the rocks without wetting his feet.

His worst fears were allayed. There was nobody inside the vehicle. There was in fact nothing at all inside the vehicle, not even a scrap of paper. The registration plates had been removed and so had the excise licence disc. The car was obviously a fairly new Audi 100 but, being upside down, access to its chassis and engine numbers was not possible.

John Grierson called to the audience of boys at the cliff top to fetch a rope from the Land Rover and throw him down one end of it. When he received the end of rope he asked the boys to tie their end to the tow ball of the Land Rover. With this done, he then led his own end beneath the Audi before tying it off to a steering arm. He then climbed to the top of the cliff and checked the knot tied by the boys.

He asked them to watch the Audi while he drove the Land Rover diagonally away from it, using the natural slope of the rocks on which the vehicle lay to pull it gently over. The boys shouted to him as it turned.

Taking a metal bar from the Land Rover Grierson flung it down to the rocks below before climbing down himself.

The metal bar enabled him to prise open the damaged bonnet of the car and finally he was able to note the chassis and engine number. He cut the rope from the car and tied it to his metal bar before climbing back up the cliff.

Andy Fleming, meantime, was spending a much more appropriate Sunday morning. He had just attended church with his wife and family and was walking with them towards the centre of town. It had been a pleasant forenoon for walking and he had decided to leave the Vauxhall at home for a change.

Some elderly members of the Congregational Church were enjoying an exchange of news in front of their church building before going home. As the Flemings passed, a voice called out.

"Constable Fleming."

Andy turned to see Aggie Fordyce, the old lady whose house shared a common close with that of Malcolm Masters.

"Why hello Mrs. Fordyce. It is nice to see you."

After the introductions had been made to Mary and the children and the usual pleasantries and compliments had been exchanged the old lady laid a hand on Andy's arm.

"My daughter told me on Friday that Fred Lord went to Paterson and McEwan that same morning with some papers. She did not pry too deeply but apparently he had been repaying a low-interest loan to some finance company and now he doesn't have to pay them anymore. He had these papers to say so. Moira just couldn't understand it."

Andy Fleming's brow furrowed. He remembered the gent in the sheepskin coat and Fred Lord leaving with the cardboard folder.

"That's very interesting." he commented. "But I don't know what to make of it either."

"Oh, and another thing." said the old lady, suddenly remembering. "Our friend Masters has someone staying with him. A smart looking chap he is too. Older than

Masters but much more refined. I can't imagine why a man like him would want to stay in a house like that."

"He's not a man in a sheepskin jacket by any chance?" ventured Fleming.

"Why yes." said the old woman with some amazement. "He does wear a sheepskin jacket and a very nice one it is."

"Is he still staying there?" Fleming asked, somewhat impatiently.

"Yes, as far as I know he is." the old lady replied plainly.

"Has he a car?" Andy pressed.

"No. He comes and goes by taxi." Aggie replied.

"Come on, Andy." Mary intervened. "Mrs. Fordyce doesn't deserve to be cross-examined on the street. Get your own answers. He never lets up, Mrs. Fordyce. You must forgive him."

"Oh, I do my dear. I certainly do."

As the family continued on their way home, Andy considered the identity of the stranger. He was so deep in thought that he almost failed to notice John Grierson and acknowledge his wave from the Land Rover as he returned from his visit to the cliffs.

The Police National Computer provided John Grierson with the registration number of the Audi car. From the registration it also provided the registered keeper of the vehicle but the owners were a Finance Company and this was Sunday. The identity of the driver might have to wait until the next day. The vehicle had not been reported stolen.

Fleming had called Colin Goodhew at Haverford and Kevin at Aberdeen with the description of the guest at Masters' house. Neither could offer any suggestion as to the identity of the man.

Colin Goodhew had some news to impart in relation to Cranston. His money had been invested with a finance company called Ransom Finance of Cardiff and the firm had suddenly folded. Cranston was not said to be too happy. A detective sergeant from Kent had been enquiring into this finance company. It was apparently connected to a few others which had closed down.

John Grierson had become impatient. It was too good a car to be at the foot of a cliff for no apparent reason. He could not wait until the next day. He phoned the police at Cardiff.

"I tell you what. The man you want is a Detective Sergeant Bradshaw of the Fraud Squad in Kent. He was in here the other day enquiring about Ransom Finance." the Welsh detective inspector advised Grierson. "Wait a minute now. I have his number here."

Grierson telephoned Bradshaw.

"Sounds like you've got my man up beside you there somewhere." Bradshaw told him. "Robert Whelan has closed MacArthur-Whelan Finance, Ransom Finance and a few others. He has made off with over a million that I know of."

"Robert Whelan." exclaimed Grierson. "So he's back up here."

Fleming's concentration was broken by the telephone ringing.

"Hello….Oh hi John. What's up?"

Grierson explained about the Audi ditched in the sea and the connection of Whelan to the car.

"This guy Bradshaw seems to think that he is up here somewhere and I'm buggered if I can think where he could be."

Fleming was no longer puzzled.

"John, get a warrant to search Masters' house for drugs. I intend to hit it at two o'clock in the morning. If you want to meet Mr. Whelan again you can come with me."

Shortly after two in the morning Malcolm Masters and his wife awoke to find torchlight shining in their eyes.

"What the hell's this?" Masters asked in something approaching a scream.

"A search warrant, Mister Masters. You didn't answer your door but it was open anyway." Fleming informed him evenly.

"A bloody search warrant in the middle of the night. This better be good. I'll be going right to my lawyer by the way."

Masters reached for a pair of trousers. His whole body shook with a mixture of fear and rage. Mrs. Masters remained in bed but mouthed her normal endearments of 'Pigs' and 'Assholes'.

The police officers worked their way through the house which was still not particularly clean or well-kept but Fleming noticed that since he had last visited the house the Masters had acquired some new possessions. A vacuum cleaner, a cooker, a fridge/freezer, a washing machine and a three piece suite stood out like sore thumbs in contrast to their surroundings. These items were still clean and smart by virtue of being recently purchased.

"Still on the dole?" Fleming asked Masters sarcastically.

"Been saving." replied Masters, matching the police officer's sarcasm.

In a jacket pocket John Grierson found a wad of notes which counted out to £2,000 in new £20 notes.

"This part of your savings too?" he asked Masters.

"That's right, man. Been saving for a wee car. Know what I mean?" Masters spoke with an edge to his voice. He had not enjoyed the discovery of this money.

The men passed finally into the spare bedroom where the bed had not been attended to since it was last used. Whelan was no longer there. Other officers had been posted outside the house in readiness for any attempted escape by Whelan but Fleming knew that they did not have him. The bed was cold.

"Who slept there?" Fleming asked.

"Me, about a fortnight ago." Masters lied. "I was legless so I was."

Fleming doubted that Masters had ever been really drunk in his whole life. A decent drink would kill him.

The pillow looked neat in comparison to the rest of the bed. Fleming lifted it up. Beneath the pillow lay a box of chocolates with a small card which said simply 'Thanks'.

"Shit." breathed Masters who had obviously been unaware of the presence of the chocolates.

"Suppose you bought these for your good lady a fortnight ago?" Grierson asked.

"Oh sure. Absolutely. She's a good wife by the way."

Fleming folded his warrant and put it in his pocket. He was quietly annoyed at being too late for Whelan.

"So you boys came up empty, eh? No dope except you." Masters gloated.

"Oh I don't know about that." retorted Fleming who had noticed the tell tale lump at the base of Masters' trouser pocket. He reached into the pocket and drew out the half ounce of compressed cannabis.

"I intend to take this and have it forensically examined. If it proves by analysis to be a controlled drug then you will have committed the offence of having possessed it. As you know that is an offence under the Misuse of Drugs Act 1971." Fleming chanted out. He held the brown lump in front of Masters' disgusted face and continued.

"As I already believe this to be the controlled drug cannabis resin I must caution you that you need not say anything. You are entitled to remain silent but if you choose to make any statement then I will take down that statement in writing and it may be used in evidence. Do you understand?"

"Yeah, yeah, yeah." Masters mimicked the chanting tone of the police officer.

"Anything to say?" Fleming asked.

"Big deal." remarked Masters and shrugged as the police officer noted his words.

"We will also keep your two thousand pounds." Fleming informed Masters. We will want to check out the serial numbers in case they are the proceeds of crime."

"That's not on." screamed Masters. "My lawyer will roast your ass, Fleming."

"Once they have been checked out," continued Fleming in a tone of polite formality, "they will be returned to your lawyer. The sum is large enough to cover his fee and leave some for yourself. Goodnight Mr. Masters."

When they had reached their own car Fleming and Grierson sat glum and silent.

After a pensive pause of several minutes it was Fleming who broke the silence.

"Where can he be, John? He has no car to give him away. Getting rid of it like that suggests that he saw this place as the end of the line for his own transport. From here on someone else helps him. I wonder if Mrs. Fordyce saw him leave. I will ask her later in the day."

After a couple of hours of restless sleep Fleming rose to resume the search for Whelan.

He checked around the hotels before any overnight guests would be leaving but he was neither hopeful nor successful. If Whelan had wanted a hotel he would have used one instead of going to Masters' house. His staying at Masters' house had to mean that the man was scared and not just scared of the law. Whelan had to be the man Loretta MacAuley had spoken about, the man who had made off with the money. The man 'as good as dead'.

Fleming thought back to the telephone conversation he had managed to record in the telephone kiosk. What had Fred Lord said? 'You could stay with me if you like, or Malky, or as a last resort there's Harry. He could take you anywhere you wanted to go'. These things had been said casually it had seemed but they had been said.

Mrs. Fordyce could not help much. She had heard someone go out of the close shortly after eleven the previous night. An engine had been running outside, waiting for the person. She had assumed that it had been a taxi and had not risen to look out.

Fleming phoned round the local taxi firms but none had picked up a fare from any Island Terrace address that evening.

John Grierson returned to the office. He had taken a run around the coast road and gone on down to Fernshaw Estate.

"How did you get on, John?" Fleming asked hopefully.

"Nothing to see down the coast road. Your friend Manson was heading out from the harbour when I was on my way back." John reported.

"Was he alone?" Andy Fleming asked.

"He was too far out for me to tell." replied John Grierson. Then he continued. "I was at Fernshaw. Kasis had Felton Lang's van. He was putting a spare wheel in it as I passed. I never saw anything of Lang himself and I never saw anything of Whelan. I spoke to the chap at the lodge. He will tell me if there is any movement."

Fleming remembered the Kasis household with its car tyres, generators, compressors, chain saws and all manner of tools. More workshop than house really. The house had been small, too small for putting up guests Fleming considered. His thoughts were interrupted as Hamish MacLeod entered the room.

"What are you doing here, Hamish? I thought you were nightshift." Andy enquired, noticing that Hamish was looking as tired as himself.

"I have the court this morning, my friend." he replied.

"Did you happen to see Felton Lang's van last night, Hamish?" Andy Fleming asked hopefully.

"Yes, as a matter of fact I did. Kasis was driving it. He came into town from the coast road."

Both Fleming and Grierson sat up in their seats.

"What time was that? Was he alone?"

Hamish was quite taken aback by the surge of interest.

"Oh here boys, steady. One question at a time. Let me see now. It would have been about half past eleven and as far as I could tell he was on his own."

"Did you see anyone else on that road?" Grierson asked.

"No. Not a soul. Just a fishing boat further down the Sound."

"Thanks Hamish." said Fleming, in a tone which also said 'well done'. "John, when you saw Manson heading out, had he come from the pier?"

"As I say, he was well out but I think by the direction of his wash he probably had been at the pier." Grierson replied.

Fleming reached for his hat.

"I'm going for a walk down the pier. See you boys when I get back."

then you will have committed the offence of having possessed it. As you know that is an offence under the Misuse of Drugs Act 1971." Fleming chanted out. He held the brown lump in front of Masters' disgusted face and continued.

"As I already believe this to be the controlled drug cannabis resin I must caution you that you need not say anything. You are entitled to remain silent but if you choose to make any statement then I will take down that statement in writing and it may be used in evidence. Do you understand?"

"Yeah, yeah, yeah." Masters mimicked the chanting tone of the police officer.

"Anything to say?" Fleming asked.

"Big deal." remarked Masters and shrugged as the police officer noted his words.

"We will also keep your two thousand pounds." Fleming informed Masters. We will want to check out the serial numbers in case they are the proceeds of crime."

"That's not on." screamed Masters. "My lawyer will roast your ass, Fleming."

"Once they have been checked out," continued Fleming in a tone of polite formality, "they will be returned to your lawyer. The sum is large enough to cover his fee and leave some for yourself. Goodnight Mr. Masters."

When they had reached their own car Fleming and Grierson sat glum and silent.

After a pensive pause of several minutes it was Fleming who broke the silence.

"Where can he be, John? He has no car to give him away. Getting rid of it like that suggests that he saw this place as the end of the line for his own transport. From here on someone else helps him. I wonder if Mrs. Fordyce saw him leave. I will ask her later in the day."

After a couple of hours of restless sleep Fleming rose to resume the search for Whelan.

He checked around the hotels before any overnight guests would be leaving but he was neither hopeful nor successful. If Whelan had wanted a hotel he would have used one instead of going to Masters' house. His staying at Masters' house had to mean that the man was scared and not just scared of the law. Whelan had to be the man Loretta MacAuley had spoken about, the man who had made off with the money. The man 'as good as dead'.

Fleming thought back to the telephone conversation he had managed to record in the telephone kiosk. What had Fred Lord said? 'You could stay with me if you like, or Malky, or as a last resort there's Harry. He could take you anywhere you wanted to go'. These things had been said casually it had seemed but they had been said.

Mrs. Fordyce could not help much. She had heard someone go out of the close shortly after eleven the

Andy walked slowly along the pier with his hands behind his back, trying to make his appearance casual and routine. It wasn't easy to conceal his impatience.

He smiled, waved and nodded to the familiar faces he saw but he was not going to be satisfied until he found Donnie MacIntosh.

At last he spotted Donnie on the deck of a visiting Mull boat, chatting to her skipper. As he saw Andy Fleming, Donnie pointed up to him as if to say 'Don't go away, I want to see you'. This was as Andy Fleming had hoped. He waited.

Donnie said his farewells to the Mull skipper and climbed up onto the pier.

"You are here to ask me 'Did I see your friend Manson today?'" Donnie said with a broad smile, "and I am here to tell you that I was hoping you would come by. The man was here this very morning and do you know he bought fuel from me for the very first time in three years."

"How much fuel, Donnie?" Fleming asked anxiously.

"Plenty." said Donnie. "Do you know he spent £260 on fuel? He had extra fuel drums with him. The bugger must be going to America."

Donnie was obviously delighted to have something to tell.

"No. Not America, but Skye maybe or Ireland or perhaps Jersey. Who knows?" replied Fleming. "He's gone now anyway. Did you see anyone else on board, Donnie?"

"No. I did not now but it's a funny thing that you should ask me that. When I was filling his tanks I saw a briefcase in the cabin. I can't imagine that scruffy bugger having a briefcase, can you?"

"Donnie, you're a marvel. I hope he paid you." Fleming laughed.

"Bloody right he did and in cash. Beautiful twenty pound notes he gave me. Come and see them, they're in my office."

The two men headed over to the portacabin that Donnie used as an office. He unlocked the office door and pulled out his cash drawer.

"There you are now. Look at these, brand new £20 notes. What do you think of that?" said Donnie, spreading the notes out on his table in a large fan.

"I think you are right, he's not alone. Before I go Donnie I want to take a note of these serial numbers. They appear to be consecutive."

"Lord bless us, Andy." exclaimed Donnie. "Don't tell me they're stolen."

"No not so much that we could ever prove. I just think they might tie in with some others I have seen."

"Oh, I see. That's good." said Donnie who didn't really see. He was just relieved not to be losing his £260.

# TEN

"Do I have to go?" Fleming asked with undisguised annoyance. "I know I said I would identify him if it would help but the poor man must have turned green by now."

"They have asked for you to make an identification as the last known person to have seen him alive. The Chief Superintendent has told them that you will go, so in answer to your question, yes, you do have to go." Chief Inspector Stewart MacKellar insisted.

"My own enquiries are at an important stage here. I can ill afford the time to go running down there to identify a Martian mummy as Frank Delby. I won't be there one minute longer than I need be." Fleming said with no attempt to hide his annoyance.

"Don't expect me to have any sympathies over enquiries that you do not see fit to tell me about." the Chief Inspector replied, making no attempt to disguise his own feelings. "I can little afford your absence from the duties I have for you but orders are orders."

"Right sir. I'll go down tonight."

GEORGE MURRAY

Fleming left the office in poor humour and went to the bus station to check on the times of buses to Glasgow. He then turned back towards the office with the intention of calling British Rail for the times of the overnight trains.

His thoughts were interrupted by a voice from a shop doorway. He turned to see the smiling face of Mr. Carmichael, the owner of the flat in the cul-de-sac.

"You asked me to tell you of any developments with the flat." he reminded Fleming. "Well it was cancelled last night. Paid in full and cancelled."

"Who cancelled it?" asked Fleming.

"The same man who rented it in the first place, Norrie Winston."

Fleming nodded his head and said nothing.

The house is clean and empty of any belongings." Mr. Carmichael added. "I went up there this morning and checked the place over. I think the person staying there must have left a few days ago. I had noticed that the curtains had not been drawn at night for several days now."

"How did you get in?" asked Fleming. "Have you a key of your own?"

"Yes I have," replied Mr. Carmichael, "but I actually used the one that Norrie Winston handed back."

Fleming thought back to the items listed by Chief Inspector Hollis as the property found on Delby's body. There had been no mention of any key and surely Delby would have taken the key when he left the house. So Winston must have been in contact with Delby after that. Had he taken the key from Delby's body or had Delby given it to him or perhaps posted it to him?

"Thanks for letting me know, Mr. Carmichael. If that man approaches you again to rent the flat perhaps you would be kind enough to let either John Grierson or myself know."

"I will be only too pleased to help." said Mr. Carmichael, touching the front of his cap as he moved away. It was a day for perfect gentlemen.

Fleming headed for the office and phoned Colin Goodhew.

"That telex from Interpol, Colin, the one about Winston being robbed in France. On what date was that supposed to have happened?"

"Just a minute, Andy."

Colin went to find the copy telex and Fleming was glad to be using the office telephone.

"I have it here. According to this the robbery was reported about 9.00 a.m. on Friday and was alleged to have happened about three o'clock that same morning."

"Yeah, I thought so." Fleming sighed. "That's the morning that Delby's body was found. Now I understand why such a robbery was reported."

"Alibi?" offered Colin.

"Alibi." confirmed Fleming. "Freshwater didn't die on the M1."

The overnight train was not especially busy but still Fleming found it difficult to sleep. He had chosen the train in preference to his own car. He did not trust the old Vauxhall to make it as far as Northampton without developing serious ill-effects.

Chief Inspector Hollis came to meet him at the station and drove him to the mortuary.

"I am very grateful to you for taking the trouble to come down." the Chief Inspector said in a patronising sort of way, as if Fleming had had the privilege of choice. "I have only the evidence of police officers who have dealt with the man in the past as identification. As you said yourself, he has no next of kin."

"When exactly was he discovered, sir? And where on the motorway was he lying? By that I mean was he in the roadway, central reservation, or what?" asked Fleming with obvious interest.

"It was shortly after five o'clock on the morning I phoned you. That was Friday, wasn't it? He wasn't discovered till daylight began to break. I would doubt that he had been lying there long, someone would have seen him. He was lying on the hard shoulder."

"The hard shoulder of which carriageway?" Fleming pressed, "North or southbound?"

"Northbound." his driver replied.

"Not near any flyovers or such?" Fleming asked.

"No. Well away from anything like that." the Chief Inspector said a little haughtily. He resented this constable from Scotland picking over the things he had considered when dealing with the accident.

They reached the mortuary and the Chief Inspector spoke with the attendants. A few moments later and Fleming was ushered in to be shown the fully exposed body of Frank Delby. It was obvious that a post mortem examination had been carried out and Fleming assumed that he was not the first police officer to view the body. Because he had been told to come down he also assumed that he was the person who knew the man best and had seen him most recently. He lifted the nicotine stained fingers of the fisherman, come seaman, come cook and looked at the red marks on his wrists.

"Wrist watch straps." explained one of the attendants.

"What watch?" said Fleming, raising an eyebrow towards the Chief Inspector.

"Is that Francis Delby?" the Chief Inspector asked coldly, obviously seeking to remind Fleming that the reason for his presence was the identification of a body and not the investigation of the death.

"Yes, that's him." replied Fleming. "I take it you have a cause of death for him?"

"Road traffic accident." the Chief Inspector said grudgingly.

"Was he wearing both his shoes when you picked him up?" Fleming insisted.

"The only shoes I ever remember seeing on Frank Delby were a pair of grey slip-ons that he had owned for years. Were they the ones?" Fleming continued.

"Yes." said the traffic officer. "I think they were."

"And he had them both on?" Fleming repeated.

"YES." the Chief Inspector said with more than a hint of annoyance.

A look of doubt crept over his face for the first time. He would not expect a pair of well-worn slip-on shoes to remain on the feet of a man battered off the road by high speed traffic in the type of road accident he had envisaged.

"Yes, they were both on." he said more quietly, almost to himself.

The attendants wheeled the body back towards the chilled compartments of the mortuary room and Fleming turned towards the door and the car he hoped would soon take him back to the railway station.

"Ready sir?" he asked softly.

"Eh? Oh yes, sorry. I'm just coming."

Driving to the railway station, the Chief Inspector remained quiet. Fleming knew that he had given the Chief Inspector cause to think. Why did the dead man still have on both shoes? He could not reconcile his idea of the accident with the fairly tidy state of dress of Frank Delby and so often before he had known tied shoes to be found yards away from the body. Dead men are unable to put their shoes back on.

Fleming did not wish to blow the poor man's mind by suggesting that dead men were also unable to untie their own wrists. Frank Delby had never owned a watch in his life.

As he travelled north again, Fleming considered the circumstances of Frank Delby's death. He arrived at the theory that Delby had been killed at some south coast port or taken there after death and thrown onto the roof of some northbound container lorry. The body had eventually fallen from the lorry on the M1.

Then again, perhaps he was simply becoming paranoid where Winston was concerned.

Manson had not spoken much to Whelan. He had picked him up at the ferry point where Kasis had dropped him. He had taken him to Flashmore and allowed him to stay. Before leaving the cottage that morning he had insisted that Whelan had handed over the promised £5,000 in cash. When he had enquired of the destination in Ireland all Whelan had said was 'Donegal. I'll tell you where to go when we get there'.

It was true that Whelan had paid for the fuel and that the £5,000 was safely at home with Manson's wife but still Harry Manson was uneasy. If Cranston came to know that he had helped Whelan then Manson might never live to spend that £5,000.

If, on the other hand, he were to dispose of Whelan, then Cranston would pay him a further £5,000. Manson slipped his hand beneath the control panel and behind the oilskin jacket which plugged the shelf. There he felt the butt end of his shotgun.

It had been placed there for reasons of defence. He would not hesitate to use it to defend himself but he had no natural disposition to violence and his thoughts of murder did not come easily. The shotgun had been retained for purposes of defence against the danger of Cranston and his men but any shooting of Whelan would be conducive to the same end.

Manson withdrew his hand but wondered if he was simply deferring an action he would have to take in the interests of his own survival. He had never been close to Whelan and was not really particular as to whether Whelan lived or died, but as long as he was living as a result of assistance from Manson, he was a threat to Manson's own life.

If he were to kill Whelan, Manson would immediately fall heir to the briefcase and the money it contained. It was from this briefcase that Whelan had withdrawn the five thousand pounds now at Flashmore and the mere fact that Whelan was taking it with him told Manson that it still held a small fortune. He looked around the cabin for the case. It had been there when Whelan was hiding in the small berth space but now it was gone. He must have taken it out on deck with him.

## THE WEED KILLER

Whelan stood on the deck behind the cabin, sheltering from the cool sea air which rushed around the vessel as it sped along, spreading a wide white wash behind it. He looked back at the diminishing shadow of the Ross of Mull and Ben More and reflected on the last twenty-four hours.

Fred Lord had advised him to stay with Masters because staying with Lord himself would have been too risky. Norrie Winston stayed close to Fred Lord and passed the house regularly. Fred Lord had asked Masters to contact Manson and arrange passage to Ireland. Fred Lord had assisted at a distance and at a price. That price had been a free settlement of a twenty grand handout from Whelan and documents which terminated on paper all the false loans previously committed to paper. Whelan had been remarkably accurate in his assessment of the man and felt proud of it. He had chosen Fred Lord as one of his clean new enterprises and Lord had grasped the opportunity with both hands. Now that Whelan was cutting out, Lord had taken no risks. Not only that, he had ensured that he could continue as an independent businessman, virtually emancipated from felonious finance and sinister obligation. From now on Fred Lord would be prosperous and revered with no need to look over his shoulder.

The same was no longer true of Robert Whelan. He was rich certainly. The money he had transferred to Dublin made him prosperous in anyone's book, but respected? No, he would need to begin all over again with new people in new places and with a new line in self-analysis to inject some substance into an ambitious but basically empty man. Living without fear was now a forlorn hope. Who could he trust? Certainly not this smelly, long haired individual who was taking him to Ireland. Masters' house had been filthy but he would gladly have stayed there for one more night if he had realised that Manson could not travel to Ireland at night without first obtaining sufficient fuel for the journey. He had been forced to stay overnight at Flashmore and to pay for the fuel when it was obtained. How could anyone live in that hovel that Manson called home? Whelan remembered the cottage when he had lived there. Manson had ruined it.

Beneath his arm Whelan's briefcase held enough money to ensure his safe passage through the Free State. People do the things you want them to do when you have money, even if what you want are the things these same people would not normally care to do. Wasn't this taxi ride from Manson evidence of that?

Money corrupts everyone, Whelan believed. Even the law perhaps, but he had not waited around to test that theory. It was quite probable that some seasoned detective was on his trail right now but less than probable that he would be waiting for him in Donegal.

The boat slowed and fell forward off the plane. With the throttle cut and the engine idling, Manson came back to fill the fuel tank.

Whelan watched him with contempt. Why should this unwashed ape have the use of a beautiful vessel like the 'Hand Maiden'? He seemed to be a good seaman certainly but so had Whelan been a good seaman. Nobody had ever given him such a vessel as this. Manson was suited to running drugs but this boat was much too elaborate. It was easy to see that Van Dongen was not at all nautical or he would not have spent so much on appearances. Manson would surely have realised that this boat exceeded authenticity but he was hardly likely to have complained.

Manson syphoned two large drums into the fuel tank and then dipped for the level. Satisfied that she could not take another drum he screwed on all the caps and headed for the cabin. He had not spoken to Whelan but he had confirmed the whereabouts of the briefcase.

As the vessel again reared up onto the plane Whelan had sensed the coldness of Manson and the need to distrust him. The way the man never spoke, the way he looked right through him as if Whelan was no longer there was a clear and callous indication that the hippy would prefer him gone. There could be no doubt that this man was doing this for the money alone. He had been paid and yet he remained silently hostile. What more did he want? More money? Manson knew that there was money in the briefcase. All he had to do was to hit Whelan over the head and take the money. He could then dispose of Whelan over the side and who would ever know? With such cause for suspicion Whelan felt that he should maintain a watchfulness over Manson. He moved to the cabin door and looked at the back of the long loose knitted garment which covered Manson almost to the tops of his Wellington boots. Whelan sensed that Manson knew he was there but the hippy helmsman stood still with his eyes firmly on the skyline.

Manson could see the Irish coast ahead but for some time now he had run towards it at a shallow angle, taking him towards the north-west of Donegal. He was buying time. In his mind he had decided to kill Whelan. He would hate doing it but it would be over in an instant. He could throw the body overboard and head for home. To hell with going ashore in Donegal, Whelan could have someone waiting to kill him and steal the boat. Whelan would have to be shot but it wouldn't be easy as long as the bugger stood behind him watching. Why was he there? Was he suspicious or was he feeling the need to be sociable?

Manson broke the silence.

"That's the Donegal coast up ahead Mr. Whelan. Do you want to tell me now where you want to go exactly?"

"You don't have to worry about that, old boy. I will take her in myself." Whelan said in clear tones of command.

"The hell you will." said Manson indignantly. "Who do you think you are?"

"I'm the man with a gun at your back." replied Whelan evenly.

Manson glanced backwards and his heart sank. It was true. The briefcase had apparently held more than money. Whelan held a small snub-nosed pistol which was pointing at Manson's back.

"Okay, you have a gun." said Manson nervously. "But that doesn't mean you need it man. I'm taking you where you want to go. There's no need to be heavy. I can take her in. Just give me directions. If I'm handling the boat, I can't give you hassle."

There was some logic in Manson's argument. Whelan could wait until the vessel was closer to its destination before he shot Manson. Whelan had the upper hand and was controlling the situation. He felt less tension.

"Just keep your hands on the wheel and take us round to the west coast." he ordered.

Manson had always relied on his wits and animal instinct and never before had they been stronger. He felt the need to buy some confidence.

"Listen man, I'm taking a real chance here. Do you know that Cranston has threatened to kill anyone who helps you and here am I taking you to Ireland?" Manson argued in what he hoped was evidence of trust.

"How do you know that?" asked Whelan, feeling no less comfortable for having his suspicions confirmed.

"He phoned everyone up and threatened them." replied Manson.

"Didn't he offer a reward for me?" Whelan asked.

"Only for information about you. Just a hundred quid. I think he wants his own people to get to you." Manson offered, trying to sound relaxed and truthful.

"Weren't you tempted?" asked Whelan.

"What? For a hundred quid? No way. Everybody felt the same. For a hundred quid it's not worth getting in touch with that man about anything. He's too wild. If the information didn't work for him he would have me shot for feeding him shit."

What Manson had said seemed probable. This sounded like the Cranston that Whelan knew.

Manson continued.

"Don't you think he might figure out you going to Ireland? He could easily get his heavies in to look for you."

"Yes. He might figure it out but his heavies are all ex-army. Most of them are ex-marines, ex British marines. All I have to do is hire some of the good old boys from the republic and tell them I am being chased by the British army. If Cranston and his mates have any sense they won't come near the bloody place."

"You really have figured it out." said Manson with a certain amount of genuine admiration in his voice.

"Just you get me in here safely and I might let you go back unscathed to that £5,000 I left with your missus." snapped Whelan as if to remind Manson that he was

## THE WEED KILLER

being covered by a gun. "And take her in closer till I see where the hell we are."

Whelan moved back from the doorway and leaned on the sides of it with both hands. He scoured the coastline but it was hopelessly distant.

"There are binoculars just inside the door." advised Manson who had sensed Whelan's predicament.

Whelan looked at Manson without speaking. The hippy appeared to be concentrating on the way ahead. Whelan reached in and took the large binoculars from the hook.

Manson did not turn his head but he took his right hand from the wheel. Ever so gently he slipped it beneath the control panel and behind the oilskin jacket. He removed the jacket and held it out from his body without turning round.

"If that spray is hitting you, you can wear this." he offered.

"No thanks." said Whelan. "Just throw it down. I'll get it if I need it."

Manson threw it backwards and put his hands back on the wheel.

They had passed Tory Island and were heading south off the west coast of Donegal.

"See anything you recognise?" Manson asked in an almost amicable tone.

"Not yet." replied Whelan. "Take her closer."

He did not wish to confide in Manson that his recognition would come from an Irish description of coastal landmarks.

As Manson steered closer to shore he realised that time for him could be running out. He slipped his hand beneath the control panel once more. The sea was a little choppy and he could not imagine that Whelan was managing to look through binoculars and point a gun accurately at the same time.

With the boat cutting the waves at full throttle, Manson's hand reached for the butt of the shotgun once more. He gripped it firmly and began to pull.

The electrical wires that Andy Fleming had threaded through the triggers began to tighten as the weapon was raised. The barrels pointed at the floor immediately aft of the bulkhead. This was the main bulkhead which served to strengthen the hull at the very part which was cutting a path through the sea water.

Eventually the wires ran out of slack and both barrels fired, blowing a hole in the hull. A 'V' shaped lip was forced downwards and the weight of sea water against it broke it off, allowing a powerful inflow of water which could never be plugged.

Manson shut off the throttle just before the vessel slewed violently to port and threw both men to the floor.

Whelan hugged his briefcase and tried desperately to regain his feet.

"Where are the lifebelts, you bloody idiot?" he screamed.

"No lifebelts, no lifejackets." Manson groaned, realising that the water was two feet high and rising.

He scrambled to his feet and waded past the struggling Whelan. Grabbing the two empty fuel drums, Manson slipped over the side of the boat into the sea.

Whelan looked hopelessly about him. The water was almost waist high and the boat would soon sink beneath him. The shore was still miles away. Manson was twenty yards astern and afloat. Whelan's despair at being unable to swim was now replaced by feelings of insult and rage at the prospect of being survived by Manson. That filthy hippy wasn't going to outlive him. Whelan took aim with his small pistol and fired repeatedly. The water around Manson turned momentarily crimson as the wounds to his head and back spurted blood. Too weak to resist, Manson made no sound as the waves washed over him.

Whelan laughed hysterically as the water reached his chest and the 'Hand Maiden' denied him her support. His laughter rang over the surface for a few moments more before the sea took all but the empty fuel drums.

Each day Manson's wife walked to the headland and sat for hours watching the seas to the south and west. Her husband had assured her that he would return that same day. Now almost a week had passed and he had still not returned.

She had telephoned Claas Van Dongen but he could not help. She had called her husband's friends Malcolm Masters and Felton Lang. They had told her that her husband might be in Ireland but had acknowledged that his going there had not been part of any plan.

Finally, she had called her parents. It had been her first contact with them for five years. Since she had taken up with Harry Manson they had not wanted to call her their daughter. She had been disowned and had responded as many another daughter would have done. She had rebelled against the wise counsel of her parents and set up home with Manson. She had happily called herself Mrs. Manson but in fact she had never gone through any form of marriage with the dope smoking, dope smuggling reprobate.

Perhaps now she was her own counsel again and in recent months she had lost the urge to be different in the way that Manson had been different. The filthy house with only the most primitive forms of sanitation and heating had lost its initial appeal of challenge and excitement. There was more to life, surely, than depriving oneself of the right to be warm, washed and well fed. Her once petite, colourful face had become pale and drawn and her figure, previously athletic and gracile was almost reduced to a skeleton.

Her parents had reminded her that a warm bath, a warm bed and a nourishing warm meal awaited her when she chose to return to them. These things waited for her alone and now she was alone, very much alone.

She would keep her daylight vigil no more.

She brought out the canvas bag she had embroidered with flowers while seated in the sunshine during those early days at Flashmore. Into it she placed a few personal items of jewellery and clothing. From the kitchen drawer she took the £5,000 which Whelan had left. She peeled off three of the crisp new £20 notes and put them into her purse beside the few single notes that Manson had given her. The remainder of the money she placed inside the front of her knickers where it could be held securely between her tights and her stomach. It felt strange to be wearing tights again. The packet had lain in her drawer since her arrival at Flashmore.

She rang the taxi firm.

She locked the cottage door and placed the key beneath the white painted stone as she had always done. If Harry were to return now he would get into the house and he would find the note she had left for him on top of the cooker, the same cooker that Ben Kasis had given her. The hens paid her little heed as she turned away and a single sob drifted off on the wind.

The ferryman watched her as they crossed.

"Still no word?" he asked quietly.

She had not spoken to the ferryman since Harry left. Yet he knew. How typical of this place.

"No." she replied in a soft but firm voice. Behind the ferryman Orsaig was becoming smaller.

The eyes of the old man passed up and down over the small, sad face, the slender clasped hands and the swollen canvas bag with its embroidered flowers. It was a vision which all but answered the questions he knew better than to ask her. Behind her he saw a taxi arriving at the ferry point.

With no further conversation they arrived at the stone steps. He helped her onto the steps as he was not waiting long enough to tie up.

She reached for her purse but the ferryman raised his hand.

"Don't want paid. This one's on me. Save your money for the taxi. Good luck to you."

She was leaving for good and he knew that too. She returned his wave and then climbed into the taxi.

For the first time in three years she was meeting people without the presence of her husband. Real people who were not part of her husband's small and duplicitous circle of friends.

"Where are you going?" the taxi driver asked.

"The bus station." she answered.

The journey was not far and the taxi driver seemed grateful for that. He rolled down his window with a speed which lacked subtlety. His passenger sat back in her seat and a tear formed in her eye. Had things really become that bad?

# THE WEED KILLER

She paid the taxi fare from the pound notes in her purse and headed for the ticket office. She took no time to look about her. There could be nobody she would recognise.

Andy Fleming recognised her and pointed her out to his companion.

"That's her, David. Looks like she's moving out."

Detective Bradshaw had been staying at a local hotel for the past two days. With Fleming's assistance he had watched for the return of the 'Hand Maiden'. From Fleming he had heard that the word around the pier was that Manson was missing at sea. He had been expected back to Orsaig on the day that John Grierson had seen him leave. Now David Bradshaw saw a sad looking woman emerge from the ticket office and walk towards the Glasgow bus.

"Let's see what she told the ticket man." suggested Fleming, moving off in the direction of the ticket office. Bradshaw went with him.

"She asked for a Glasgow single journey ticket." the ticket clerk told the police officers. "Bought it with a new £20 note."

He drew the note from his cash drawer.

Both officers looked at the note and saw that the serial number was close to those they already had on their list. The ticket seller watched this examination with great curiosity.

Bradshaw took out his wallet.

"Do you mind if I take this note and give you two tenners in its place?" he asked the curious official.

"As long as your tenners are dry." the ticket man joked. "I don't mind."

"Thanks." continued Bradshaw. "By the way, did she say where she would be going to from Glasgow?"

"Not exactly, but she is going for a train. She asked how far it was from the bus station to the Central Railway Station." the ticket man remembered.

"Mmm. Sounds like she's going home." Bradshaw said quietly, almost to himself. "Back home to her parents, a rich but abandoned wife."

"Or a rich widow." Fleming offered.

As the half empty bus pulled out, the frail and tearful girl placed her hand on the bulge of her abdomen. She wondered how she would make her explanations to her mum and dad. The money could be explained easily as her husband's earnings or savings but the young life beginning to form behind the money was a secret that Manson himself had never known. She had been looking forward so much to telling him.

A heavy tear dropped from her cheek onto an embroidered blue flower.

"Are you finished here now, David?" Andy Fleming asked the man with the task of tracing Whelan.

"I still have to go to that Ballinbuck Hotel and get statements regarding the sale of it by Whelan to the present owners. Perhaps they could help with suggestions as to where he might have gone. Are they to be trusted Andrew?"

David Bradshaw was a perfect gentleman and a thorough investigator. Fleming would have enjoyed the opportunity to have worked with him more often.

"I couldn't say much about them I'm afraid. The Ballinbuck Hotel is in someone else's area altogether. A word with the local cop would be worthwhile though. I have spoken to him before and I know that he keeps an eye on the place."

"Good." said Bradshaw. "Then I shall head back south to see if Mrs. Manson is going to her parents' home as we suspect."

"Good luck." said Fleming as the two men shook hands.

Fleming watched Bradshaw drive off. He had given the English detective the name and address of Mrs. Manson's parents. Fleming just hoped that no-one ever asked where he had come by it.

# ELEVEN

Another two weeks passed and still nothing was seen or heard of Robert Whelan, Harry Manson or the 'Hand Maiden'. Fleming and Grierson had discussed the mystery several times and asked around the pier and the island. Nothing new had emerged. Detective Superintendent Naismith had been told of the circumstances and he had passed the story on to the Customs.

Fleming and Grierson met yet again in the muster room of the Police Office to compare notes.

"Don't suppose Felton Lang or Benjamin Kasis have much business at the moment." John Grierson suggested.

"Felton Lang was in Edinburgh yesterday." replied Fleming.

"How do you know that?" asked Grierson.

"He got caught for speeding on Ferry Road. The traffic guys phoned through to check out his address." said Fleming.

"I thought I saw Lang's van going into Fernshaw this morning." John Grierson commented.

"Yes." said Fleming. "Life goes on."

"Do you think they are still running drugs?" big John asked.

"Of course." said Fleming emphatically. "Why else would Lang's vehicle be in Edinburgh? He has no other reason for going there and no other reason for entertaining Aberdeen guys in his home."

Fleming had given himself cause to think. He rose and walked to the window. As he watched the good people of the town going about their business he continued.

"Bradshaw phoned me this morning. He was just checking that Manson had not returned. He knows that Whelan drew £25,000 in new £20 notes. The serial numbers are known. The money he gave Masters and Donnie MacIntosh came from that lot, so did the note Manson's wife used to buy her bus ticket. She has gone home to her parents and apparently now looks more like a normal person. She had deposited £4,500 in cash with a building society. These notes were also from Whelan's twenty-five grand."

John Grierson leaned forward in his chair.

"Surely he can question her about the whole business." Grierson reasoned. "He has the money as definite proof of her involvement with Whelan."

"I suppose." agreed Fleming. "But the money was really being paid to her husband. Outside of that she would not necessarily know anything. Besides, the twenty-five thousand was only pocket money for immediate expenses. Whelan had transferred whole accounts, amounting to well over a million pounds. Bradshaw has traced them to Ireland. To Dublin in fact, but so far nobody has come near it. No more of the Bank of England £20 notes have turned up and Bradshaw is giving them time to surface from the Irish banking system. He won't be approaching anyone for a while yet. In the meantime Mrs. Manson doesn't seem to be going anywhere but the ante-natal clinic."

Grierson gave a short ironic laugh.

"Poor bitch. Nae luck." he commented.

Fleming remained silent for a few moments. He was watching Loretta MacAuley go into a small tobacconists shop across the street.

"I'll be back in a minute." he told Grierson and he left the office by the rear door.

Fleming waited down the street where he knew he could not be seen from the police office windows. Loretta saw him from a distance and she smiled. It seemed obvious to her that he was waiting to speak to her.

"Well kid, you engaged yet?" Fleming asked with a smile.

"No. Davy says he's thinking about it though." she replied, laughing. "That means you still have plenty of time to save up for my wedding present."

"What does Dave make of this Manson affair? You do know that he has disappeared, boat and all?" Fleming asked in a quieter more serious tone.

"Yes. I never heard about it from Davy, right enough, but I asked him about it. He said it would be the same man that did it before. I asked him what he meant but all he said was something about a Frenchman being a killer."

Loretta was being honest, she had heard no more.

"I don't like asking him about these guys, Andy." she continued. "He gets nervous and he doesn't want to tell me. If I ask him too much he gets angry."

She had said this as if to discourage Fleming from pressing her to discover more from Davy.

"He cannot live in fear forever." Andy Fleming advised. "He can talk to me anytime and privately if he wants, just as long as he's not involved himself."

"No. He's not so stupid as to be involved and he hates their guts but I know he won't talk to you, Andy. I've tried. I really have." she said with a tone of hopelessness.

"Okay kid, don't push it." said Fleming. "But let me know anything you hear. Take care and remember.... I'll be watching for that diamond."

He moved back towards his office.

"See you." she said softly.

He half raised his hand as he turned away.

He did not feel like going back to the police office immediately. He and Grierson would only get locked in discussion over points they had covered so many times before. Such discussion would only serve to highlight the funereal pace of their enquiries.

The mysterious disappearance of Whelan and Manson had drastically altered matters from the past few months when isolated incidents and new characters had produced such intriguing furcation to their lines of enquiry. The two main characters had dissolved and left Fleming temporarily set back in his purpose. He wandered off on quiet side streets, uncertain for the time being of everything but his desire to be alone.

When he had walked for some considerable time he found himself looking over the back wall of the Fire Station yard, instinctively questioning the banging sounds from behind the wall. He saw his friend, Kenny Murdoch, the Station Officer, throwing various items into a large metal skip. Fleming went in to join Kenny.

"What's this Kenny? A bit of spring cleaning?"

Kenny Murdoch turned and swept his forearm across his brow.

"It's yourself, Andy. Want a job? Just look at this lot. For months now I've been promising to clear out these old storerooms. This is me suffering for putting it off for so long."

Fleming looked into the skip.

"You've got all kinds of everything in there, Kenny. Are you sure it's all rubbish?" he teased.

Kenny laughed.

"Hey, don't be saying that. It's getting to the stage when I just feel like throwing the stuff out without thinking. That way I'll be finished quicker. Look at this place here. Have you ever seen so much junk?"

Fleming looked into the dark storeroom and saw that it was filled almost to the ceiling with old equipment.

"Hard to believe that you could accumulate this much." remarked Fleming. "There's a large hose there. What's wrong with it? Is it burst?"

"It's old and parts of it are frayed," replied Kenny, "but I don't know that it is actually burst. When they get to a certain age and condition we have to take them out of service. You could have it if you have a use for it."

"What could I use such a big hose for, Kenny? It must be four or five inches across." laughed Fleming.

"Yes." agreed Murdoch. "And fifty metres long. The boatyards sometimes take the reinforced ones to use as supporting straps when they are craning boats out and in the water."

"Ah. That's a good idea." said Fleming, adopting a more pensive look. "And I have just thought of an even better idea. Pat Craig at the lifeboat pier has a problem with the lifeboat hitting against the pier wall in rough weather. The tyres are not enough, for the boat is thrown against the wall at different heights, above and below the tyres. This is damaging the hull."

"I know what you mean, Andy. That wee boat of mine is the same. In rough water, fendering is difficult. What had you in mind?"

"I think I could paint your hose white, for the sake of appearance, and then Pat and I could fill it with sand.

We could suspend it down the pier wall in deep, close set loops between the mooring posts. It would be heavy but Donnie Grant would give us some old chains to hang it with. Once it was in place we could decorate it a little, in the lifeboat colours perhaps." Fleming suggested, feeling and sounding rather proud of himself.

"Sounds like a good idea," said Kenny, "and a lot of work. I'll put it over by the gate. You can pick it up later. It'll take time to paint it and fill it with sand, a lot of time."

"I might just manage to find the time the way things are." said Fleming without expecting Kenny Murdoch to appreciate the significance of the remark. "I'll give you a hand to carry it. It looks pretty heavy."

Fleming was really quite excited by his idea. The prospect of providing some original and tangible contribution to the lifeboat service pleased him and brought some light relief from the mental maelstrom of his drugs enquiry.

He had realised that he would need the kind of paint which would stand up against the rough sea wall and remain unaffected by exposure to salt water. He had also realised that such paint might not come cheap. Only when he consulted the ships chandlers did he realise how right he had been. The stuff was extortionate. He only bought white paint.

Over the next couple of days he spread the hose out over the top of his garden fence, a length at a time, and painted it. He cursed his luck for having to visit the chandlers shop a further twice in order to finish the job but he was pleased with the end result.

Once the job was done and the paint was dry he rolled up the hose and put it in the boot of the Vauxhall. On his next day off he would deliver it to Pat Craig and they could make a start to the business of filling it with sand.

The late shift was no joke. Every afternoon from Easter to September, the west highland policeman becomes a tourist guide. For the most part the questions are repetitive and expected.

"Excuse me. Where are the toilets?"

"I say officer, can you recommend a place to stay?"

"Hey buddy, where's the Greyhound station?"

Difficult to answer or not the unusual questions were welcome and interesting.

"Are there any massage parlours?" a German enquired.

"Where can I buy a castle?" asked an American.

"What is a Jersey fishing boat doing in your harbour?"

Andy Fleming stared down at the little man with the camera. He was from Whitby.

"What kind of Jersey fishing boat?" Fleming asked back.

"A big orange trawler." the holidaymaker replied. "I wouldn't have thought she would be this far north."

"They fish the Atlantic, sir. Sometimes much farther north than here but you're right. They don't often have much cause to call at our ports. Perhaps the weather or some minor repair."

Andy could not get away from the tourist quickly enough. He walked to the pier as fast as decorum would allow.

The 'Moon Vixen' was easy to see. She was bright orange and huge. Fleming looked her over from bow to stern. There did not seem to be anyone aboard now that she was tied up, berthed three out from the pier. In the sunlight that blessed that afternoon, Fleming could make out her every detail. Something about her bow drew his attention. Big and powerful though her bow was, it was sheathed in lead for the full length of the main bow stem. Like the boat, the bow was painted orange but the odd scuff had exposed the grey lead colour beneath. Fleming could not understand why such a thing should have been done.

Behind the wheelhouse there was an accommodation block with a door towards the pier. This door opened and a big man emerged onto the deck. He stopped briefly as if to adjust to the sunlight before climbing over, onto the next boat and again to the next, making his way to the pier. His bearing was that of a skipper.

## THE WEED KILLER

He was powerfully built and he had a deep tan. A thick cigar protruded from the centre of a dense, black beard.

As he walked past the police officer the fishing boat skipper was not looking at anyone in particular. Even so, Andy Fleming thought he must be the most evil looking man he had ever seen. He watched the skipper walk to the telephone kiosk at the end of the pier and make a telephone call after consulting a small notebook he took from his pocket. The call lasted but a few moments and then the bearded man returned.

This time, as the man approached, Fleming spoke.

"Bonjour, monsieur."

The seaman looked a little surprised but no more pleasant.

"Bonjour." he growled.

Fleming wondered. Could this be the French killer that Davy had told Loretta about? He returned to the Main Street and walked round by the Drypuddle Bar just as Benjamin Kasis came out.

"Well Ben. How are you lot making out? Still enough gear to go round?" Fleming said a little sarcastically.

Kasis gave a dry laugh and waved one finger from side to side.

"Yeah. Enough to go round. That's neat my man. That's what it's been doing, goin' round man." Again he laughed.

He took the keys from his pocket and headed for the yellow van parked further up the street. Fleming returned to the police office and made a couple of telephone calls.

Colin Goodhew was able to confirm from the description given by Fleming that the bearded man was Jacques Troutam, skipper of the 'Moon Vixen'. He was unable to explain the lead sheathed bow of the trawler.

About seven o'clock in the evening Troutam came ashore with four other men. He met Norrie Winston on the pier and all six men walked off in the direction of the Argyll Crest Hotel where they entered the public bar.

Fleming watched with interest. The bar was licensed until one in the morning. He hoped that the crew of the 'Moon Vixen' would make full use of the drinking time available.

Darkness fell around quarter to ten and by eleven o'clock, when Fleming finished his shift, the pier was dark and deserted.

He drove home and quickly changed into his black attire. He tied the small inflatable dinghy to his roof rack and drove to the shore road on the opposite side of the pier.

Equipped with a sharp, short bladed knife, a retractable tape measure and a small torch he set off in his dinghy, quietly paddling through the darkness towards the giant shadow of the Jersey trawler.

Keeping to the seaward side of the boats he knew that he would remain virtually invisible to anyone on the pier. He followed the hull of the 'Moon Vixen' forward until he grasped the lead sheath which covered the bow.

Very slowly and tentatively he stood up in his dinghy and held onto the trawler's bow as best he could with his left hand. Fortunately for him the water was calm and little support was needed to stabilise himself.

With the knife in his right hand he stretched as far up the port side of the bow as he could and cut into the soft lead. Slowly, but with all the strength his wrist could achieve he cut downwards through the lead. He cut right down to water level before placing the knife out of harm's way. Still standing and riskily using both hands, he peeled the lead forward and back away from the cut itself, revealing the bow stem beneath.

Fleming took the small torch from his pocket and examined the original bow.

From a height of approximately five feet down to water level the bow was badly damaged. Not so badly as to be a danger but certainly bad enough to draw attention and speculation as to how the damage had been caused.

Large splinter sections had been broken out of the main stem and similar pieces, while broken, still remained in place. Where the planking of the hull met with the stem, deep scoring, almost horizontal, had taken place.

Against the bright orange paintwork there were other paint scores. Black paint had been impressed onto the orange by impact. Fleming had seen this sort of paint transfer before in cases of road accident damage.

Looking more closely, Fleming found a black painted splinter embedded in the grain of the trawler's hull. The black splinter could not be pulled out but Fleming managed to break it off. He put it in his pocket and took out the retractable tape measure.

The top of the damage was fairly obvious and fortunately for the 'Moon Vixen' that was where the damage was worst.

Fleming pulled out the metal tape in excess of his estimate and held the tape vertically downwards against the bow until the beginning of it just broke the water's surface. He then noted that the upper limit of the damage was five feet and three inches above the surface. Returning the tape and torch to his pocket, Fleming began to squeeze together the edges of the lead. He realised that the damage he had caused would be discovered as soon as the boat went to sea, when the force of the water would push the lead apart. That could not be helped.

Quietly he pushed and pulled his way back along the trawler's hull with arms that ached from the exertions of the previous five minutes. When he had almost reached the stern of the vessel he heard the sound of someone coughing, someone just above him on the deck of the 'Moon Vixen'.

Fleming froze. He had assumed that all had left the boat to go ashore.

The man on deck coughed once more. It was a coarse cough, a smoker's cough which cleared the throat of phlegm. He then spat overboard and the weighty deposit struck the water just two feet from the dinghy. The fisherman then gulped noisily before releasing a belch like musket fire.

Andy Fleming pulled his dinghy round the stern of the fishing boat and soon realised that he had been right to do so for no sooner had he moved round the stern than a beer can was thrown into the water and pouring down on the spot Fleming had just left, the unmistakable sound of an emptying bladder.

Fleming paddled away, wondering why Troutam had considered it necessary to leave a guard on board. What was he guarding?

Looking around the boats moored to the pier, Fleming found the 'Eilean Belle' and paddled up to her stern. He had wanted to go alongside but she was alongside other boats and for that reason he was obliged to go aboard. He tied the painter of his dinghy to a stern cleat and clambered aboard, taking his 'tool kit' with him.

He quickly noticed that the port side provided a gap of several inches between the 'Eilean Belle' and the similar vessel outside of her. Fleming pulled out his tape measure to a length of five feet and three inches and held it vertically down from the top of the side rail of the 'Eilean Belle'. He found that the bottom of the tape reached, or just broke, the surface of the water at that height when measured from the part of the side rail just astern of the wheelhouse. This would be a 'blind' spot for the helmsman and an area where a broadside impact would almost certainly cause an immediate capsize of the vessel.

With the sharp knife, now not quite as sharp, Fleming cut a wedge of wood from the gunwale rail of the 'Eilean Belle' at this part behind the wheelhouse, making a silent apology to the friendly old skipper as he did so. He purposefully put this wedge in the opposite trouser pocket from the splinter broken from the bow of the 'Vixen'.

Returning to his dinghy he paddled towards the coast road and he was a much relieved man when he reached the old Vauxhall.

On his way home he parked some fifty yards from the Argyll Crest Hotel and walked to the front windows of the public bar. He looked over the lower opaque section of the window and saw that Winston, Troutam and company were in fine form in the centre of the busy bar.

It was a quarter to one in the morning. Fleming looked around the car park, then returned to his car. As he drove off he saw Davy Russell, the worse of drink, staggering towards the hotel. Loretta wasn't with him and for Davy it was just as well.

## THE WEED KILLER

It was a fine dry morning as John Grierson walked to the village shop for his morning paper. As early as this, a little after eight, the shop was never busy and John spoke for several minutes with the elderly couple who had run the shop for more years than John had known.

As he made his way back home he glanced at the bungalow owned by Norrie Winston. He gasped aloud. In the time he had spent at the local shop he had missed the arrival of the brown Rolls Royce. He walked home without staring at the car but telephoned Fleming as soon as he got in.

"Aye. They're the same all right. Mahogany too. You could never afford that standard for side rails nowadays. Beautiful wood. You would be lucky to get it at all now, even if you could afford it. These pieces could be from the same boat. They might even be from the same bit of wood. This is the modern equivalent over here. You'll see the difference."

Donnie Grant was in no doubt. The samples were identical in age and origin. It was as Fleming had suspected.

"Was Davy in here last night, George?"

The barman at the Argyll Crest could see that she was more concerned than annoyed.

"Aye, he was, but he never got drink from me, Loretta. I put him out. He was steamin' and if I hadnae put him out these guys would have killed him."

Loretta was no less anxious.

"What guys, George?"

"The guys from the Jersey boat. They were in here last night with that chap from the fish lorry, Norrie something or other." George began. He didn't want to go on, but the look on Loretta's face told him that only the whole story would do.

"They had been in all night and word must have got about. It was nearly closing time when Davy came in. Like I said, he was miraculous drunk. He started shouting at the big chap with the beard, accusing him of murdering Jamie Cameron. The big guy didn't understand what Davy was saying but he wasn't too happy at Davy shouting at him. I went over and grabbed Davy. A couple of the regulars helped me put him out."

"Then what happened?" Loretta pressed.

"That Norrie chap must have heard what Davy had said. He came over to me and asked who Jamie Cameron was. I just told him that Jamie had been lost at sea a few years back." George said in little more than a whisper. "Then he said 'How does he reckon my big mate killed him?'. I just told him that Davy must think that the big boats were forcing the smaller boats to take more chances."

"What did he say to that?" asked Loretta.

"He just shrugged his shoulders and went back to his mates." replied George. "They spoke among themselves and then left together."

"Yeah, and Davy hasn't been seen since." sighed Loretta.

Andy Fleming came back to the office in good heart. The identification of the wood samples by Donnie Grant meant almost conclusively that the 'Moon Vixen' had collided heavily with a fishing boat of identical size and form to the 'Eilean Belle'. This must surely mean the 'Beacon Belle'.

Hamish MacLeod and Ian Pearson were waiting to give him more good news.

"The police at Aberdeen phoned for you." said Hamish. "They have Benjamin Kasis in custody for possession with intent to supply. Guess where he had the gear."

"In the tyre of the spare wheel." said Fleming confidently.

"Aye. That's right. How did you know?" asked Pearson.

"I told them where to look." said Fleming. "I asked Kasis if he had enough to go round and he nearly split his sides laughing. That more or less confirmed what I had suspected...."

"That the stuff was going round in a wheel?" Pearson interjected.

"That's right. Remember when we raided his house under warrant he had all these tyres lying around in the workshop? Remember he had all the gear for fitting tyres and blowing them up?"

Pearson nodded.

"Very few of them were the right size for that old van he used to have. The better ones were a different size from his vehicle but they were all the same size. I took a note of that at the time but only recently did I think to check the size of these tyres against the tyre size of Felton Lang's van. I wondered why the van went to Fernshaw as often and then big John told me he had seen Kasis putting in the spare wheel."

"Well, you were right." said Hamish cheerily. "There was almost six pounds of the stuff inside that spare tyre."

As if the atmosphere was not euphoric enough, John Grierson stuck his head round the room door to say, "Hey, anybody in here want to see the Rolls I've just seen being parked near the pier?"

# TWELVE

"I've never been so glad to see a piece of road finished." said Des Urquhart. "I was sure that some of us would get killed before this job was done."

"Aye, you're right, Des." agreed Sam MacDonald. "Still it's finished now. The crazy buggers can kill themselves if they want."

Des Urquhart had been the ganger of the road squad which had just re-surfaced the road over the railway bridge. He stood on the grass verge and looked back at the work they had done.

The main road south followed a parallel course to the railway but the railway then cut deep into the rock in order to take a steep decline to the level of the lochside. For the past ninety years there had been a stone bridge to carry the road across the railway, one hundred feet above the gorge. It was here that the road took a sharp left turn around a bluff of rock in order to cross the bridge at right angles.

The heavy traffic and the winter frosts had badly damaged the road surface on the approach bends and on the bridge itself.

Drivers who did not know the road very well were inclined to assume that it would continue in the fairly straight manner in which it had followed the railway. The bends onto the bridge from either direction were inclined to catch out those who travel too fast and in recognition of this the roads engineers had provided white sidelines for the carriageway. These lines had proved to be a great success but in the course of re-surfacing work these, like the old surface, had been completely removed.

Vehicles travelling so fast as to overshoot the bend would require to be caught in the roadside ditches and small trees to avoid leaping into the deep railway gorge below.

By strategic placing of signs and traffic lights the workmen had managed to keep the speed of traffic to sensible levels but even so Des Urquhart had seen too many close things for his own peace of mind. Hardly a day had gone by but one of his men had jumped into the rhododendron bushes at the side of the road to escape some heavy footed maniac in a sports car or a late-for-dinner touring coach.

The new black surface looked sound enough but without the side road markings that had been there before. All white lining stopped just before the bend.

"That will be risky at night until the white lines are painted in again." remarked Des. "I'll phone the roads engineer when I get back. In the meantime, Sam, you better put up these 'No Road Markings' signs and leave the 'Road Works' ones. That might be enough to encourage the buggers to slow down."

Donnie MacIntosh watched from the cab of his fuel tanker as Troutam left the 'Moon Vixen' to climb up to the pier. Waiting for him there was an even bigger man, dressed in a shiny beige suit. Even from a distance Donnie could see that this man had gold rings on most of his fingers and he wore expensive looking shoes.

Troutam shook the man's hand and together they walked towards a brown Rolls Royce which was parked near the entrance to the pier. Norrie Winston waited in the passenger seat of the car.

A hundred yards away the uniformed figure of Andy Fleming watched Cranston and his henchmen with even greater interest. He had watched the Rolls Royce from the time John Grierson had told him of its arrival in town.

"Why was Cranston here?" he wondered.

Two possibilities occurred to him. Either he wanted to be present for the return of Whelan and Manson or he knew that they would not return and Manson would not be available to play any further part in the illicit import business. It seemed to be the absence of the 'Hand Maiden' which had forced the 'Moon Vixen' into port. Even the worst weather had never forced her into doing that. Fleming remembered the guard posted aboard her the previous night and felt fairly sure that the trawler was on drugs business as usual. What would Fleming not give to hear the conversation in that Rolls Royce?

Cranston and Winston left the vehicle and walked across the street to a licensed grocer's shop. A few minutes later they came from the shop carrying two large cardboard boxes which appeared to contain something heavy. The boxes were placed in the car and the contents were shown to Troutam before they were taken out again and placed in the boot. The men drove off but only as far as the Argyll Crest Hotel. The vehicle was locked up and the three men surveyed the menu contained in a brass case beside the door of the hotel.

Fleming headed for the off-licence where the manager was a personal friend. Fortunately the shop was free of customers.

"Okay Smithy old son, what can you tell me about these two big guys that just left?"

"My best customers today." replied Bobby Smith with a smile and a rub of his hands. "They bought six bottles of spirits, six dozen cans of beer and just about every other drink you can think of. The guy in the brown suit paid for them from a wad of notes that would choke a horse. I asked them if they wanted Coke and they laughed. 'Said they had plenty already."

"Did they say anything to you or to each other besides ordering the drink?" asked Andy.

"The big guy insisted that I put the order into two big cardboard boxes. I went through the back to get the boxes and I heard them talk between themselves. I heard the big man say 'We'll put the stuff into these boxes later'. The other chap said 'When are we leaving?' and the big man said 'About three in the morning'. They spoke about somebody called Jack and the big man said they would take him."

"Was that all?" Fleming urged.

"Yes, that's all that was said, Andy. I'm pretty sure."

"Thanks Smithy. You've been a real help."

Bobby Smith acknowledged the half raised hand of the police officer.

Cranston was holding court at the table in the corner of the dining room. Even to those who did not know the men they must have appeared to be a mafia group in conference.

"This will be the last that this place sees of us." Cranston told the others. "If Manson is dead then we will have to move north and use Brunton. I don't like him. He drinks too much but he's all we've got until I can get somebody decent into that area."

"Why go so far north?" asked Troutam.

"We've talked about this before." replied Cranston. "We have to go north to get away from the Customs and the police. On this coast there's hardly a soul and no big towns at all. It stands to reason that there isn't hundreds of police and Customs just waiting for the odd bit of dope. If we tried to come ashore further south we would be taking a far bigger risk."

"I do take risk." said Troutam, a little indignantly. "The sea is bad here, sometimes very dangerous."

"That's what you are getting paid for. You don't think I would be paying you the kind of money you get if you were only paddling ashore at Morecambe?" growled Cranston.

"All right." said Troutam submissively. "I take big risk....and big money."

The three men laughed at this and raised their glasses to toast their continued prosperity.

"Superintendent Naismith please."

Andy Fleming looked anxiously at the clock. He knew that Larry Naismith was not one to hang about after five o'clock.

"Hello sir. Andy Fleming. I think we will have something to go for tonight."

He then related the recent developments and the information picked up by Bobby Smith.

"It looks as if they're heading south during the night with the stuff." Andy concluded.

"Can you not take them before they leave?" the Detective Superintendent asked.

"I don't think that would be a wise thing to try, sir. For one thing we don't have the resources and for another I believe that these men will probably be armed. If they are in a car and a hundred miles into their journey they will be less alert or apprehensive in respect of any police activity." Fleming argued. "Besides, up here there are seven or eight of them. I think the car will only hold two or three when it leaves."

"Why do you think they are armed?" the Superintendent enquired.

Fleming admitted that he had known of Manson keeping a shotgun on the 'Hand Maiden' for protection against Cranston and his cronies.

"Well, in that case." Larry Naismith said slowly, obviously considering what to do about the threat of firearms. "You will have to keep me posted as to when they leave, how many there are and which road they are using. I'll be in touch with Bill Symon at the Scottish Crime Squad. We'll get ourselves organised at this end."

"John. You'll need to help me on this one. I can't follow Cranston out of town at three in the morning and hope that he doesn't clock me. My old car would stick out like a sore thumb and if he went at speed I would lose him."

John Grierson looked a little annoyed at Fleming for inferring that he needed to ask. Grierson would never have forgiven him if he had not expected John to take a willing part in this particular piece of action.

"What have you in mind?" John asked, leaving no doubt as to his commitment.

"I want to wait out country as far as I can and when he arrives I'll follow him at a distance until I can be sure of his route. Once I know that I can phone through to Symon or Naismith." Fleming explained. "Cranston won't suspect an old Vauxhall from one of the villages heading south with only one passenger."

"Sounds good. I suppose you want me to tell you when they leave here. How can I do that?" Grierson asked.

"Yes. I'll phone in from a suitable kiosk and leave the number at the office. When Cranston leaves here you can go to the office and phone me. That should give me plenty of warning. I'll be parked by the telephone kiosk, waiting for your call."

Fleming sounded confident. He knew that in John Grierson he could not have a better accomplice.

Both men asked to be excused from wearing their uniforms that evening and together they walked to the pier. On their way there they noticed that the Rolls Royce was still at the Argyll Crest Hotel.

They met Donnie MacIntosh and asked his permission to sit in his portacabin. From there they could watch the 'Moon Vixen' in some comfort. Donnie was waiting to fuel two large Moray Firth trawlers which were due in at midnight. He was only too glad to enjoy some company.

"The 'Saint Margaret' and the 'Moray Alice' are big boats," said Donnie, lighting a cigarette and pushing his packet towards John Grierson, "and big customers for me. They were here in the early hours of the morning and they left again when they couldn't get me on the phone. I was up at my daughter's. They left me a note through the office door there to say that they would be back at midnight to fuel up for the trip north."

"This is their night for landing, is it not?" Grierson asked. "They usually manage to fully load these two Glasgow lorries between them."

"Aye, that's right." confirmed Donnie, "but you only know that because the lorry drivers give you some of that fish for a fry."

They all laughed and began to recount amusing anecdotes of fish gained and lost. The time began to pass more quickly.

Shortly after eleven o'clock the men saw the brown Rolls Royce drive noiselessly onto the pier. It turned and stopped opposite the 'Moon Vixen'. The three occupants got out and the door of the accommodation block of the 'Moon Vixen' opened. One of the crew looked out expectantly.

Cranston and Troutam lifted out the boxes from the boot of the car and Cranston gave his to Winston before closing the boot lid. The three then made their way to the boat with hoots and guffaws of laughter which suggested that they had already consumed a fair degree of alcohol at the hotel.

"I better get going, John." said Fleming. "They might leave early."

"Yeah, right. Remember to phone in the kiosk number or the plan's buggered." big John reminded him.

With his customary half raised hand of farewell, Fleming slipped out into the night. Skirting the piled nets and boxes he made his way invisibly to the pier entrance.

He stopped to look around for his old Vauxhall and his attention was drawn to a figure leaning over the sea wall. In the poor street lighting he could make out that this was a young woman and in the still night air her sobbing easily reached Fleming's ears. He moved closer and recognition came to him. It was Loretta.

"Loretta, what's wrong?" he asked quietly.

Loretta turned slowly. Her reddened eyes stared at Andy for a second before she threw herself forward and put her arms around him.

"Oh Andy, Andy." she whimpered. "I think they've killed Davy."

"What do you mean, Loretta? Who's killed Davy?" asked Fleming, pushing her gently back until he was looking her in the eye.

"These men from the Jersey boat." she answered, looking towards the 'Vixen'. "He accused them of murdering Jamie Cameron and Davy's not been seen since. I've looked everywhere. Nobody has seen or heard of him since last night."

Fleming remembered that he had seen Davy heading for the Argyll Crest Hotel.

"Was this in the Argyll Crest that he accused them?" he asked.

She nodded her head and resumed her crying.

"They followed him out of the bar. He was drunk and alone. He's dead I tell you."

Fleming looked sideways at the 'Vixen'. Would they hang around if they had killed Davy? With these people the answer was uncertain.

He placed his hands on the sides of Loretta's face and looked into her eyes.

"That was only last night, Loretta. Davy has lots of friends. Someone has taken him home. He'll turn up, I'm sure he will." he whispered with strained sincerity.

"Yeah. I'm sure too. Sure he'll turn up floating in that harbour." she said angrily.

Fleming put his arms around her and squeezed her gently.

"We don't know that lass. Not yet anyway. I've got to go now but as soon as I get back I'll start looking for Davy. Okay?"

She nodded against his chest. Fleming kept his arms around her and squeezed her again. He knew the pain of losing a good friend.

He left her to watch over the harbour.

To make up for time spent with Loretta he drove quickly on the southbound road, trying to put as many miles as possible behind him before finding some suitable telephone kiosk.

The road was deserted and dark. The front of a filling station, closed but lit up, provided the only illumination. The old Vauxhall flashed in and out of the fluorescent light and continued for another mile before reaching the railway bridge.

Andy Fleming knew that the road curved sharply to his left and crossed over the railway. He saw the road signs warning him of road works and a lack of white lining but he was almost caught out by his speed when the road turned black and the guidelines disappeared.

He braked hard and then released the brake before steering round to his left, successfully holding the proper course.

Three miles farther on, he found the roadside kiosk he wanted. He parked beside it and telephoned the police office to leave the number for big John.

Fleming looked at his watch. One o'clock. He could expect to wait another two hours before following the Rolls Royce south towards Glasgow. He would have to be patient. He had a full tank of petrol in readiness for the journey but he might need some of it to fuel the heater in the meantime. It was a clear crisp night.

As he lay back in his seat with the heater fan blowing warm air at him he considered the number of times he had spent time and money of his own to keep tabs on the Cranstons, Langs, Allisons and Mansons. Only now were the city slickers on expenses ready to move their butts. Now that the bad guys were rounded up and put on a plate, the cavalry was going to arrive. For Fleming's part he was on his own time again, even at this late stage. He had paid for his petrol to follow these guys and he would not even be there when they were caught. To the 'glory boys' would go the glory. They would make the arrests and to the press that is what would matter. The arresting officers would also earn the admiration of the Assistant Chief Constable. Arrests in themselves are relatively cost-effective.

Fleming remembered how he had thought of Kevin when someone else arrested Allison.

Fleming did not want the glory but he did want to get these men. He thought back over their behaviour as he knew it and considered their behaviour as it had been suspected. He thought of Loretta and her sadness. She could well be right about Davy. What if she was right? What would happen to these guys? Five years? Ten years? Who could believe that they would ever be adequately dealt with in Loretta's eyes? They were evil men devoid of conscience but how much conscience had justice itself?

Realising that his mind was racing ahead of events Fleming gave his head a shake and looked sideways at the silent kiosk and then at his watch. Ten past one.

At the pier the 'Saint Margaret' and the 'Moray Alice' had berthed. As one landed her boxes of fish, Donnie fuelled the other.

John Grierson continued to watch the 'Moon Vixen'. Now that he was alone his eyes were inclined to drop shut. It had been a long tiring day. His forehead touched against the cold glass of the window and he jerked awake. Cranston and Winston were on the pier, placing the cardboard boxes in the boot of the Rolls Royce. Troutam was stepping up onto the pier with a long parcel under his arm. The parcel had a covering of sackcloth wound around it like a bandage. As Troutam reached the car one end of the sackcloth slipped and revealed the ends of the barrels of two shotguns. The parcel was placed in the front passenger seat. The three men boarded the vehicle and Cranston set off at speed. John watched them go with a feeling of relief. He was no coward but these were evil men and if they were to become desperate they would also become merciless. He thought of Andy Fleming isolated on the long dark road and he gave an involuntary shiver.

John Grierson left the portacabin and waved to Donnie MacIntosh before slipping away quickly towards the police office. As he left the pier he saw the lonely silhouette of Loretta MacAuley moving slowly onto the pier. There was something doleful and worrying about the way she looked but Grierson had no time to spend on anything but his phone call to Fleming.

When the telephone rang it surprised Fleming. It was earlier than expected.

John Grierson told him that the boxes had been placed in the boot and that two shotguns were being carried in the front of the vehicle.

"Keep your distance, Andy. If these guys get suspicious, they'll just blast you." cautioned Grierson.

There was an uncharacteristic note of caring in the big fellow's voice but the presence of firearms changes most things.

"John, do me a favour. Phone Larry Naismith or Bill Symon and give them all they want to know about this car and the firearms. I will phone them from somewhere further on along the route but you had better warn them about the guns. Don't worry about me. I'll back off as soon as I know which way they are going." Fleming said with a haste and inflection which betrayed his excitement.

"Right Andy. Good luck."

Grierson put down the phone and struggled to remember a telephone number he could normally dial without thinking twice. His mind was already midway through his report to Larry Naismith.

Fleming jumped back into the old Vauxhall. One thought was uppermost in his mind.

"They had guns."

He had told Larry Naismith that they might be armed but he had hoped to be wrong. He had told Loretta that they had not killed Davy. Who was he to suppose that he was right and she was wrong about that? His mind went rapidly back over his past knowledge of these people. He thought of Manson and Whelan, of Frank Delby, of 'Sponge' Catterson, of the damaged bow of the 'Vixen' and what that told him of the 'Beacon Belle'.

He had no right to believe that it had finished. He could be next, although he had no intentions of taking that risk. To leave Mary a widow and his children without a father at the hands of scum like these would be unforgivable. But his was not the only life he was putting at risk. After all his efforts he, Andy Fleming personally, could be creating an incident in which someone else might die. These young men he had been accusing, in his thoughts of an hour before, of seeking glory from the capture of Cranston, could just as easily be despatched to Glory by that same low-life individual. Would Fleming feel any less responsible for their widows and orphans?

He had created the danger. The responsibility for the events of that night would be his and the blood that would almost certainly be shed would be on his conscience. If these evil killers drove past him now he would be powerless to do anything but wait to hear how great would be his burden of guilt. He was destined to carry guilt. It was he who had roused the beast which would slay his colleagues and only by slaughter could the beast be stopped. He was alone and out of uniform.

He was unarmed and the odds were impossible but there had to be a way.

He spun the car around and headed back the way he had come. He crossed the railway bridge and parked at the edge of the northbound lane, keeping his engine running and his dipped headlights switched on.

Taking a sharp knife from the glove compartment, he ran to the opposite side of the road and began to cut through the stems of some smaller rhododendron bushes. Once they were loose he returned to his car and opened the boot. He lifted out the reel of white painted hose, intended for the lifeboat jetty, and carried it with difficulty to the point where the sideline of the southbound lane had finished. He placed the loose end of the flat hose on the end of the existing line and held it there with his foot before pushing the reel towards the far side of the road, beyond the apex of the bend. The far end of the hose dropped over the edge of the tarmacadam surface and into the narrow ditch beyond.

Taking the loose rhododendron bushes, Fleming placed them to the left of the straight hose reel at irregular intervals. This gave the impression of a continuation of the natural roadside.

He returned to the Vauxhall once more and brought a pair of binoculars from the passenger seat. He climbed up the rocky bluff far enough to be able to see for a considerable distance in both directions.

The road was clear of traffic with the exception of one southbound vehicle, still some distance away but travelling fast, appearing to Fleming as no more than a pair of headlamps. It was vital that he be sure. He concentrated on the roadway where it crossed in front of the filling station.

The vehicle was only lit for a second but that was long enough. It was the brown Rolls Royce. Fleming quickly looked to the south for traffic from that direction but he saw none. He returned to his vehicle.

As he saw the headlamps of the Rolls Royce approach from a distance Fleming switched his own headlamps to full beam until the Rolls was closer then he dipped them and drove forward at a crawl. He hoped to create the impression of a northbound vehicle travelling over a length of straight road.

Cranston gripped the steering wheel firmly and he occasionally glanced down at the speedometer. He was finding it easy to drive fast on this empty road. His powerful headlamps gave him ample warning of any change in direction of these white lines which bordered the road.

His life was all about ego and he had spent it impressing and intimidating other men. He was prepared to be marginally reckless at times in order to gain the respect of other big, powerful men like Winston and Troutam. He was driving his car at a speed that they suspected of being in excess of his ability, causing them to fidget and glance at each other. Cranston noticed this and was comforted by the feeling of superiority it brought him.

In the distance he could see the headlights of another vehicle, the first he had seen since leaving town. For some time the oncoming lights were mildly annoying. Just as Cranston was about to curse them, they dipped.

With his attention on the approaching car he failed to see the warning signs left by Des Urquhart.

Maintaining his seventy miles an hour, Cranston flashed past the old Vauxhall and his vision, temporarily impaired by the first headlights of the night and the alcohol he had consumed, accepted the straight white line with gratitude. He neither braked nor swerved.

The heavy car rose from the cambered bend like an aircraft from a carrier and sailed over the ditch, over the bushes and over the rylock fencing. It succeeded in passing over everything that had previously prevented vehicles from reaching the gorge.

For Cranston, Winston and Troutam the world was no longer a real place. The engine noise was suddenly audible, the swish of tyres on dry road was not. Their senses became a vicious vortex with impending doom the only instinct left to them. The headlamps made no impression on the cloudless sky but they clearly lit up the rock faces to either side of the gorge. The railway line passed upwards before them as the car somersaulted.

Landing on its roof a hundred feet down did nothing but harm to the appearance of the classic car and on the railway line the three big men had made no impression at all. All three had flown straight to Hell. As if to confirm their destiny, the Rolls Royce burst into flames.

Fleming looked down at the inferno for a few moments with mixed emotions.

He took no pride in what he saw. This had always been a war and in a war people get killed. He took some comfort from the knowledge that the grieving relatives would not be those of his colleagues. The deaths of these men was his sin and he would keep it in his heart, just as he had kept his promise.

His composure slowly returned and he gathered in his hose. The rhododendron bushes were put back in place and he drove back to the kiosk.

"Hello John. Just to let you know that nothing has passed me here. I doubt Cranston has met with an accident. I'll backtrack and see what's happened. I'll be in touch."

Loretta kept her head down as she walked past the trawlers at a distance.

She had wanted the pier to be deserted and lonely, just like her. It was not part of her nature to feel depressed but she had fallen as low in spirit as she had ever been. It had always suited her happy-go-lucky style to believe that her feelings for Davy were something over which she had complete control. Now that her feelings were cornered by his disappearance she began to realise that she truly loved him. That realisation may have come too late. She was sure that Davy was in the water and lost to her forever.

The men loading the fish lorries were too busy to notice her. Their north-east accents rang through the still air and chased the sad Loretta away. Why was everyone so busy? Even Andy Fleming had been too busy to listen.

She reached the quiet end of the pier and sat down on some fish boxes to stare at the water. Only now did she realise how much Davy really meant to her. Only now, when it was too late.

The last of the fish was swung ashore and a young fisherman climbed out of the hold to ask the skipper, "Want me for anything else?"

The skipper laughed.

"Fit wid a want wi' a drunken loon like you?"

The whole crew laughed. It was obvious that the skipper was not being serious.

"Aye, you've done weel." the skipper said as he reached for his pocket. "Here, tak this fir yir help and if ye come aboot the 'Moray Alice' again ye better be sober. I'll maybies let ye bide if ye are."

The young man climbed up onto the pier and looked at the four ten pound notes he had just been paid for twenty four hours on the big trawler. He noticed Donnie MacIntosh locking up his portacabin.

"Hey Donnie. How about a lift up the road?" he called.

His voice carried along the pier to a small pile of fish boxes. Loretta turned her head.

"Davy? Davy Russell is that you?"

Fleming was back at the office. He had told John Grierson of the fire he had 'discovered'. The railway authority had also been told. Now he told Naismith.

"Yes sir. It is a bad bend at any time but normally the vehicles leaving the road would be caught up in the bushes or fences if they clear the ditch but he was travelling so fast that he cleared everything"...."About twenty miles out."...."Yes the end of the line for Cranston."...."Telex? Yes I'll see that you get a copy of the telex sir. There'll be one to have the relatives informed. I'll see that Colin Goodhew gets a copy of that."...."Right sir. Thank-you. Goodnight."

The small church was looking its best in the afternoon sunshine. Fleming stood on the wide concrete path and admired it for a few moments before walking slowly towards the door.

It was several weeks now since the old minister had retired and the church had not been in use. The occasional tradesman had been in to attend to matters in readiness for the arrival of the new minister and the resumption of Sunday services. For that reason Fleming paid little attention to the small blue car parked at the far side of the vestry.

It surprised him a little to find the front door open but it pleased him that the place seemed prepared to welcome him. There had been very few sounds outside, only birds singing, traffic passing, but inside there was total silence. It was also cooler. Not cold at all, just cooler. The vertical stained glass windows along the side of the building threw shafts of light across the tops of the pews and revealed a million dancing dust particles.

Fleming closed the door behind him and moved slowly down the red carpet of the aisle until he reached the pew he would normally occupy on Sunday mornings. He sat down, clasped his hands across his knees and bent his head forward until his forehead rested on the bookshelf in front of him. He considered the way things had happened over the previous three years and the part he had played to influence events. He thought of the hardship he had placed on his wife through a craving to deal with a problem that was universal but had been adopted by him for a personal crusade. He had not only devoted time and energy to his crusade. He had devoted his own money and Mary had been the poorer for it. He had been judge and jury over all those involved in the drugs scene; and he had been a harsh critic of people who were responsible for tackling drugs enquiries on a much wider scale than his; and ultimately he had been more than a crusader, he had been an avenging angel.

Fleming twisted his hands together and his face took on a pained expression. He was no angel. He had promised himself revenge. He was a law officer who had stepped outside the law. He was not merely satisfied to bring the guilty to justice, he had to be the one to define that justice.

It was true that the deaths caused by Cranston and his henchmen could never be proved beyond doubt. They could scarcely be counted beyond doubt. It was true that, if the deaths and other miseries could be proved, then the punishment by law would be woefully inappropriate.

Fleming had adopted a responsibility which had never really been his and in his own mind he had jealously maintained the right to deal with the matters he had exposed. He had carried this to the point of deciding and administering the penalty. He had been so wrong and now he knew it.

He sought forgiveness for his mistakes.

As he raised his head he saw a fresh faced young man standing in front of the altar, looking at him. The man wore a sports jacket and flannels but the clerical collar was what caught Fleming's attention.

"I would hope to see more faces on a Sunday morning but this is very encouraging." said the young minister, stepping forward with outstretched hand. "I'm Andrew MacCallum."

"Andrew Fleming."

## THE WEED KILLER

Andrew MacCallum explained that he had been invited to fill the vacant post and had come to see the church before coming to any decision.

"My friends have been accusing me of taking early retirement. I certainly don't agree with them but if they had said that I was leaving the rat race I might be less inclined to argue. This does not seem to me to be the kind of area where people could be capable of much sin. What do you think, Mr. Fleming?"

"Weeds can appear in any garden Mr. MacCallum."

"Aha." said Andrew MacCallum, enjoying the analogy. "So we must dispose of the weeds before they spoil the garden, eh?"

"You make the point too well Mr. MacCallum."

The whole rotten business was over and in the cool of the early evening Andy treated Mary to a walk along the shingle beach. She enjoyed this walk so much but he had never found the time to share it with her for over a year.

"Pat Craig likes my idea." he told her, throwing a stone towards the sea. "We will start to fill the hose tomorrow."

"That should keep you out of trouble." Mary remarked, taking his hand. "I don't expect that you intend to get up in the middle of the night to put sand in a hose?"

"No, certainly not." Fleming laughed.

"Oh, by the way Mary, we have a wedding present to buy."

"Who for?" asked Mary.

"Loretta." he said as if she would know who that was.

"Who's Loretta?" she asked.

"The girl who is marrying Davy." he replied.

"And who is Davy?" she asked a little suspiciously.

"Davy is a fisherman." he said teasingly.

Mary still imagined that she should be able to reach a point of recognition. She placed the forefinger of her free hand across her lips and looked down at the pebbles pensively as she walked.

"I know." she said at last. "Davy is the chap who was at school with you. The one who used to write you all these letters."

"No dear," Fleming said sadly, "that was Fergus, Fergus Morrison."

The author is retired but his professional life was spent in law enforcement. An operational career in Scottish police forces was followed by roles in private health security, aviation security, civil law process and Scots Law proofing.

He is a husband, father and grandfather and now resides in Edinburgh.